'*The Organised Criminal* is a masterly novel of male friendship, family betrayal and economic corruption. By turns brutal, beautiful and funny, it's an astute exploration of an Ireland rarely seen in fiction.'

—Jamie O'Neill, author of *At Swim, Two Boys*

'Jarlath Gregory's *The Organised Criminal* has themes which are familiar – family, betrayal, love and death – but the setting and the characterisations and the telling of the tale make this a distinctive and fresh book, one that can read like a thriller but linger like something much more dangerous.'

—Keith Ridgway, author of *Hawthorn & Child*

Published in 2015 by
Liberties Press
140 Terenure Road North | Terenure | Dublin 6W
Tel: +353 (1) 405 5701
www. libertiespress. com | info@libertiespress. com

Trade enquiries to Gill & Macmillan Distribution
Hume Avenue | Park West | Dublin 12
T: +353 (1) 500 9534 | F: +353 (1) 500 9595 | E: sales@gillmacmillan. ie

Distributed in the UK by
Turnaround Publisher Services
Unit 3 | Olympia Trading Estate | Coburg Road | London N22 6TZ
T: +44 (0) 20 8829 3000 | E: orders@turnaround-uk. com

Distributed in the United States by
Casemate-IPM | 22841 Quicksilver Dr | Dulles, VA 20166
T: +1 (703) 661-1586 | F: +1 (703) 661-1547 | E: ipmmail@presswarehouse. com

ISBN: 978-1-909718-93-7
2 4 6 8 10 9 7 5 3 1

A CIP record for this title is available from the British Library.

Cover design by Karen Vaughan – Liberties Press
Internal design by Liberties Press

The Organised Criminal

Jarlath Gregory

LIB
ERT
IES

This book is dedicated to my parents, Tim and Josie,
with gratitude that they are nothing like Frank and Dolores

1

Wake

The journey home was barely an hour long. My only travelling companions were fat middle-aged men in business suits, discussing high finance in loud voices. One of them flicked through a newspaper, which I read over his shoulder. Job layoffs at a factory in the midlands. Dublin taxi drivers protesting over new legislation by blocking the roads on a Saturday morning. A mother strangled in front of her kids. Ho hum.

He turned the page and I saw my cousin's face.

SMUGGLING SUSPECT FOUND DEAD

Duncan Goodman, 23, from South Armagh, Northern Ireland, was found dead at his apartment yesterday. He had died as a result acute liver failure. Mr Goodman was suspected by authorities on both sides of the border of being involved in the lucrative smuggling industry based near his native Crossmaglen. The funeral will take place in his hometown on Thursday.

I was going home for the wake. My coffee came with two thin paper tubes of sugar and two small plastic tubs of milk. The movement of the train made the cup wobble. A dribble of coffee soaked into a disposable napkin, but at least the coffee was strong and hot.

The international news was devoted to war.

The bombs of my youth, the ones which had exploded a mile or two away from my house, killing the soldiers whom it was my father's business to evade, had given way to other wars, other cultural grievances, with other people's financial interests at the heart of the injuries, maimings, and death. I imagine all civil war unfolds in the same way. It begins with a bloody dispute over land, an unjust division of the spoils, an occupied people with a genuine cause to fight for. People in power take the best of what there is to plunder and those without power struggle to survive, until the bright, idealistic, angry men join forces to rebel.

They recruit muscle, attack breeds counter-attack, groups fragment and splinter according to their political bent and thirst for blood, until both sides build up enough mythology to breed a younger generation, who can't remember where it began, but know for a fact it's the other side's fault. Meanwhile, industries thrive on keeping the two sides locked in war, the perpetual stalemate kept artificially alive by those with vested interests in staving off a resolution until, eventually, the perpetrators grow rich enough to call the violence to a halt, and claim credit for building a process of peace.

I needed a smoke.

Duncan had always been keener on the family business than I was. He'd worked for my father since he was sixteen, starting as a lookout and clambering his way up the ranks to messenger, delivery boy, and finally a runner, until his drinking got out of hand.

What did he have to show for being a cog in the wheel of organised crime? An ex-wife who'd sucked up one black eye too many, two kids he wasn't allowed within one hundred yards of, and a shitty flat to drink himself to death in. My cousin had always been weak. He'd finally cracked. And now he'd done Frank O'Reilly a favour and killed himself with booze, which meant that I had to go home and face my dad for the first time in three years.

I leant my head against the window, catching the double reflection of my three-quarter profile in the inner and outer panes of glass. I looked like any other student returning home from university. I'd cut all my ties when I'd left.

There hadn't been many to begin with. University had been a chance to start from scratch, because in the city, you could be anyone. At least now, I'd get to catch up with Martin. It had been too long. I missed him. I let my thoughts drift to an image of Martin, red-haired and sunburned, kicking a can at a burnt-out lorry, which drifted into an image of Martin, in a ripped T-shirt and Doc Marten boots, dancing on top of a police car in broad daylight, which drifted into an image of Martin, toolbelt slung around overalls, casually blowing a kiss at one of the guys shouting abuse at him.

The sweep of other people's towns continued beyond the window of the train, offering glimpses of lives lived by the train track, behind windows of their own. A lone tree sweeping sideways along an exposed slice of coastline caught my eye, its image staying in my mind long after the coastline turned into a ruined castle, a bridge above a town, a housing estate. It leant at what ought to have been an awkward angle, not upwards, but sideways, sloping as if caught mid-dance. It was beautiful, singular, a thing of nature, but also a product of its environment. All trees in unprotected areas grow crooked according to the prevailing wind. Maybe they're even more beautiful because of it.

I closed my eyes to the world outside and tried to close my ears to the loud, fat bankers who had fucked up the country. No matter where you were, you couldn't escape the necrotic stench of money, corruption and our zombie economy.

The train heaved into Dundalk station.

The yellow-bricked station gleamed like butter under an aged glass canopy. Old-fashioned black-and-white photos of days long gone were displayed alongside windows that offered glimpses into a small museum of historical railroad artefacts. It felt, for more than one reason, like stepping back in time. I hoisted my sports bag onto my shoulder and trudged up the steep slope out of the station. The space had won awards for its innovative use of printed poetry on glass, which now sat chipped upon its panels like the nail varnish of a polite, ageing punk.

Once, the heady smell of hops would have wafted over the car park from the adjacent brewery, weaving its alco-holic breath through the crowds of workers and shoppers returned from the capital. It had recently been shut down, its glass and steel keening silently against the carefree clouds in a clear blue sky. I got a taxi.

'How am I supposed to make a living if they open up the taxi market to every Tom, Dick and Harry from here to Nigeria? It's hard enough making a living out of this job without them blacks coming over here and setting up shop.'

The crooked little shops I remembered from my youth

were gone, replaced by estate agents (closed), mobile-phone stores (open), and delicatessens (struggling, by the looks of it). Pristine outcrops of half-finished apartment blocks lay dormant on the outskirts of town. A burst football lay in the overgrown grass of a house that gleamed like someone's dream. Somewhere, a dog barked. No signs of life flickered behind the windows of the empty homes.

'They're so dark in the skin, you can hardly see their faces above the steering wheels.'

Everyone wanted someone to blame, and the lower you were to the ground, the more you kicked against the people beneath you. You'd swear the world had ended because Joe and Mary could no longer afford Louis Vuitton wallets for their credit-card receipts, never mind their brief, exalted positions as petty landlords to the plebs. I let him rant. If it wasn't for passengers' earholes, he'd be clogging up the national airwaves on phone-in radio shows.

'I used to be able to take two holidays to Majorca every year. Now I'm lucky if I can take a week off to visit the in-laws in Carlow. Or maybe not so lucky, what? Haha.'

As for me, I was a little worse off with the extra tax hikes eating into the wages from my part-time job in a bar, but the real kicker was what to do after graduation. People were still drinking, and barmen still needed to pull pints, but I didn't want to do that all my life. Most people I knew were emigrating. The dole cuts were designed to send students packing.

'So I said to the missus, there'll be no extension this year or next year love, no point in talking to me about putting up the value of the house. Sure who can afford to buy a four-bedroom gaff with or without a bleeding conservatory at the minute, anyway?'

The car's suspension took a jolt. The smooth tarmac had given way to a crumbling mess of uncared-for stone and tar, trundled and crushed beneath the wheels of largely illegal commerce, destined to be repaired by neither the Irish nor the British authorities.

We were in no man's land, the border, bandit country.

'Just here, please, on the left. No need to drive through.'

The taxi driver stopped mid-anecdote and assumed a neutral expression.

'Tenner, pal.'

I didn't leave a tip. I waited until the taxi driver had pulled away before punching in the code to the wrought-iron gates, which, luckily, hadn't been changed since I'd been gone. 24-04-19-16, the first day of the Easter Rising.

Our house was unmistakably a smuggler's house, as the taxi driver had recognised. It had been built slap bang on the border, half in the North and half in the South, in its own nest of land and outhouses. The bricks were oxblood, the pillars were marble, and the windows were bulletproof. My family home was three storeys of ostentatious, unashamed, recession-proof wealth. My dad must've had someone in to landscape the lawn. I couldn't have named a single one of the shrubs or plants lining the driveway, and I'm sure he couldn't either.

The crunch of gravel beneath my trainers reminded me of the marble chips on graves.

I rang the doorbell.

Heels clicked on the marble floor.

A shadow moved across the eyehole in the door.

The door swung open. My mother stood in the hallway, making mourning look almost indecently glamorous. Dolores O'Reilly swooped upon me, enveloping me in an enormous hug. I gave in to it, as you do, as she planted lipstick kisses on my face.

She drew back, examining me at arm's length.

'I always knew you'd come home. Eventually.'

It wasn't as if we hadn't seen each other since I'd left home. She frequently visited me in Dublin for tea and sandwiches and superficial conversation at one swanky hotel or another. With a careful finger, she fixed her miraculously un-smudged mascara free of a single tear.

'You should've called, but I'll put it down to inconsolable grief. If your good suit is in that,' she said, pointing at my sports bag, 'we'll have to have it pressed.'

I stepped over the threshold, and nothing changed.

'Hi mum,' I said, awkwardly kissing her cheek.

Dolores drew a fingertip over her cheekbone, as if I'd slapped her and it stung. Her fingers and wrists glinted with gold jewellery.

'When's the funeral?'

'Tomorrow. Look lively, we have to show our faces at the wake. Go make yourself presentable. Have a shower, and I'll iron your shirt.'

She paused, drawing a finger across my collar.

'Such as it is.'

The main bathroom had been done up. I stood on the unfamiliar tiles and stripped. Bits of me were reflected in the chrome and mirrored fixtures. The steam billowed from the shower and I stepped in, the water stinging my face, thinking about the last time I'd been in a church. It had been for someone's wedding, when I was just a kid. I remembered being squeezed between Dolores and Frank as the photographer fiddled with the million buttons on his camera. I'd shifted from one patent leather foot to another. A fly had rubbed its eerie little paws together on the white carnations on the altarpiece. A bead of sweat had trickled down Frank's face as he tried to hold a smile. Dolores had gripped me by the elbow with a painted talon, and told me to quit squirming and try to look happy.

I already knew that marriage was bullshit. From the priest saying his magic words, to the Christmas dinner we ate at the height of summer in the big, ugly, expensive hotel afterwards, to the posed pictures in clothes we never wore, it was all bullshit. Everybody knew it, but they pretended not to.

Most people were hypocrites, and I was no different.

I showered, shaved, and put on a shirt and tie.

Dolores drove us to the wake. We both smoked until we got there.

Duncan was being waked in his mother's semi-detached home. Dozens of cars were parked in and around the labyrinthine innards of the concrete estate. Kids with plastic toys played on the kerbs, oblivious to death and its aftermath. I flipped down my sunshade and looked in the mirror. My eyes were anxious. My palms were sweaty.

Weddings, funerals, what was the difference?

I prepared myself for duty.

My mum calmly straightened her necklace, applied another layer of lipstick, and patted her hair.

'Look lively.'

I flicked my smouldering cigarette butt into a ditch. It

had once been a laneway between neighbouring estates where kids from either side of the divide had come to wage mock wars, but it had since been cleaned up, landscaped, and fenced off. A peeling piece of graffiti spelled 'IRA' in bottle green, off-white, and burnt orange.

Dolores walked briskly ahead. The first person we met at the door was Duncan's brother Seamus. We'd never got on.

'Seamus, I'm so, so sorry, where's your poor mother?'

Dolores sailed onwards, leaving me to shake hands awkwardly with my cousin.

'Jay, long time no see. Get yourself a drink, man. I'll catch up with you later.'

The usual herd of extended family milled in and out of rooms. I caught glimpses of familiar faces, those faces you only ever see at weddings or funerals. There'd be time enough for conversation later. I went upstairs to pay my respects.

All the blinds in the house were drawn. Plates of sandwiches and tea were doing the rounds, attached to various capable women, the sort of women who always seemed to be at wakes. I could smell the whiff of booze from downstairs. I braced myself to walk through the door to Duncan's old bedroom.

The room was crowded with mourners, interspersed with the tricks of the Catholic trade – candles, holy water, a priest. Weird, that there was still a market for all that holy tat. The murmurs died for a second as I entered the room, then picked up again, slightly louder than before. Dozens of pairs of eyes took me in while pretending not to.

I stared at the coffin. It lay lengthways across the room, side-on as you entered. It was mahogany with brass fittings.

It was open.

While silk ruffles cushioned the dead, sewn-shut, made-up face of my cousin. Duncan looked both bloated and drained, if that was possible. It made sense when you realised he'd been bloated by booze before death, and drained of blood by the embalmer afterwards.

A wad of padding had come loose from one nostril. Someone ought to fix it, in case Duncan's face leaked, in case that became the last image I'd ever be able to conjure up of my cousin – the spongy face, leaking brain sewage through its nose, down its drawn lips, dripping from the chin. But I couldn't bring myself to reach across and touch the body.

Like everyone else, I pretended the dislodged nose plug wasn't there.

I stepped forward.

Several bodies melted away in deference to a relative of the deceased.

I forced myself to look down upon the face of Duncan Goodman for the last time. I clasped my hands together in what I knew the room would take for silent prayer, although no prayers came to mind, only a contemplation of the dead.

My earliest memory of my cousin was just an image, sun-bloomed, hazy, and faded round the edges like an over-exposed photo from the Nineties – which it was, in a way, except it had been recorded in my brain, as a young child growing dimly aware of the strange world I was part of. I was six and he was seven. Duncan stood chest high in over-grown grass, grinning with gaps in his teeth, blond curls made dark by the sun dancing over his shoulders. A home-made jumper, knitted by Aunty Kate. Freckles. If I tried too hard to focus on the picture, my cousin's face would morph into an older version of itself, the teeth crooked and stained, the hair sparse and colourless, the cheeks and nose mottled with alcohol, the eyes smashed and gluey like broken eggs.

The room returned.

Light filtered through gauzy curtains.

The wreaths around the coffin were scentless and sombre. I said goodbye to Duncan and tried to focus on the normal things. The chink of china teacups borrowed from the football club. The rough fabric of the black chairs brought by the funeral home. Shuffling shoes, clasped hands, the solid chill of a house with the heat turned off, both out of respect for the dead, and the practical necessity of keeping the body cool.

All part of the great Northern Irish theatrical tradition of the family wake.

At first, I didn't hear the voice at my ear.

'Jay? Jay? Cup of tea, Jay?'

My cousin Scarlett thrust a laden tea tray under my nose.

'Have a cup of tea, you'll feel much better.'

'Thanks.'

'I've put a drop of whiskey in it, just for you,' she whispered.

I accepted the concoction gratefully.

Scarlett's thin wrist bones made the china look clumsy. She was wearing a Claddagh ring, turned inwards to show she was engaged. I hadn't seen one of those in years.

I looked up into her face, surprised.

She smiled back brightly and widely.

'Come outside. We could both use some fresh air.'

Everyone gave way to the tea tray.

Scarlett nodded at two smokers in the backyard and perched on top of the coal bunker, plonking the tray down on its sloping lid at a disarming angle. We sat in silence. I lit a cigarette and blew smoke rings at the sky. A crackling spool of film played across my mind, a film of the last time I'd seen our cousin alive.

Duncan had been living in a dingy council flat, the kind he used to take the piss out of people for being from. Newry had improved since we'd been to school there – it now had coffee shops as well as shopping centres, stellar hotels as well as self-service petrol stations, successful drug-dealers as well as rat-arsed pubs – but the old slums still slumbered amid the glass-and-chrome complexes, sleeping alongside the vroom and tinkle of the coin-operated car-parks, ignored by the twinkling clamour of the bells of the cathedral, which always conjured up images of confetti and doves fluttering through the air, even as smog slipped through your hair.

If you squinted just right, the haze of a weak summer sunlight filtering through pollution might make the rooftops, windows and traffic shimmer like any British high street, with international brand names punctuating the depressing local muddle of the markets, the undeveloped outskirts, the sink estates. Up close and personal, sectarian graffiti dripped off peeling walls. Mums pushed prams past half-cracked beggars, greeting them by name with weary tolerance. Tracksuits were the uniform of the non-working classes.

And it was here, in the midst of the squalor and decay, up the inevitably piss-soaked stairway, past the same laundry hanging on the same balcony with the same child crying in the background that I remembered from my daily walk to school three years ago, that my cousin had drunk himself to death.

'Nice place. It's good to have your own flat, right?'

'It's OK.'

Duncan had kicked an empty can across the room, flopped down on an armchair of indeterminate colour, lit a cigarette, and offered me the packet. I'd taken one, resisting an impulse to seize Duncan's wrist to stop the tremor in his hand, and lit my cigarette off the tip of his one. The flat was a kip, but what did you expect?

'So Her Majesty's paying for all this?' I said, spreading my arms wide to encompass the tax-payers' bountiful gifts unto the humble recipient of social welfare and sickness benefit, in recognition of his being too gravely ill to hold down any position of gainful employment.

'Good scam, being on the sick. Rotten roof over your head, British money in your hand, cheap drink down your neck. Wouldn't want to get dry and lose all this, right? This is the life.'

'Do you want to get dry?'

'I do in me arse.'

'Go home much?'

'More than you. Still working in the pub?'

'Yeah.'

'You must get a fierce amount of drink for free. What's the price of a pint in Dublin these days?'

We'd talked about booze, cracking open Duncan's medicinal stash of cans one after the other, until he began to repeat himself. I kept drinking to drown out the sound of soap operas, dance music and barking pit-bulls, as dusk blushed against the open, staring windows. In the distance, on the hill, our old school winked in the neon-lit evening. I'd left him there, drooling on the sofa.

Still, I hadn't realised how close he was to killing himself with the booze. You don't expect someone in their twenties to lie down and die.

'Lost the run of himself completely,' I'd said to no one in particular, taking in the view from the communal stairway, and spitting over the railings.

The smokers tossed their cigarette butts to the ground, where they bounced and smouldered like spent bullet shells. The noise of children from the estate rose above the wall. Pale light bled the concrete white. It was nice, sitting there with Scarlett. We were almost the same age and we used to be close, but as I'd left home and she'd stayed behind, I only saw her on Facebook these days. A fly landed on a slice of cake. Scarlett idly pressed her thumb on top of it, squashing its body into the moist crumb.

'You know what I call this dense fruit-and-vanilla flavoured sponge?'

'Shock me.'

'Wake cake. You only ever get it at wakes, and no wake is complete without it.'

Scarlett wiped her thumb off on her jeans.

'Let's go back and see if we can force this slice on Fr Flaherty.'

'Deal.'

Scarlett slid off the coal bunker, put on a smile, and picked up the tray. Her Claddagh ring caught a glint of sunlight.

'I didn't know you'd got engaged.'

Before she could answer, a banshee wail rose from the scullery. Aunty Kate came wobbling out into the yard, arms outstretched, fresh tears pricking her eyes.

'Jay, you came home, you came home . . .'

I met her outstretched arms in an awkward embrace, then held her to my chest as she sobbed, while men looked at the floor, and the smile faded from Scarlett's lips, the tea tray growing heavier in her hands.

Back indoors, I found myself clutching a whiskey. I could already see the nosey aunties mentally making tallies of how much I'd had to drink. It was a drunkard's funeral, and all they had to look forward to in their parochial little lives was the next one. Why not give them something to talk about?

Men, loud and fat, backslapped each other. I poured the shot straight down my throat, and poured myself another. The whiskey stung the back of my eyeballs.

The men were smugglers, or business associates of my dad, if you preferred to see it that way. Frank O'Reilly had run the family business, namely the lucrative cross-border smuggling industry of South Armagh, for four decades.

It was one of those elusive facts of life which everyone believed but nobody could prove, like the existence of dark matter.

'They call this bandit country,' he would grunt, 'but the only bandits round here are wearing British army uniforms.'

I'd always known that you weren't supposed to talk about it. I brushed my teeth, washed my face, went to school, and didn't talk about it. I played chase, did my homework, kept my head down, and didn't talk about it. I kicked a ball around, shared a cigarette, kissed a girl if I got the chance, but still, I never, ever, spoke about my dad's business.

'Rule number one,' Frank drummed home, 'we don't talk about it. That's how we get rich, and stay rich.'

Rich. Yeah, we were rich, but we didn't brag about it. Instead, we wore it in a certain swagger, in a winter tan and a smattering of Spanish, in never having to explain ourselves, because, just as I never talked about my dad being a smuggler, nobody else did either.

'Son.'

I spun around.

My dad stood in the middle of the room, like a bullock in a black suit.

'Come with me, Jay. I need to have a word.'

The room fell silent. This was the moment that everyone had been waiting for. The whiskey burned a hole in my belly. I did as I was told. I followed my dad out of the room, through the crowd, and into the estate. A child was pouring a can of beer into the gutter, where cigarette butts floated like dead goldfish in a pissy pond.

2

Money

There'd been no major bust-up the last time I'd seen my dad. We'd never had the sort of relationship where we'd yell or throw fists at each other. In fact, we'd never said much to each other at all.

It had been silently understood that Frank was preparing me to take over his business when he was gone. I knew how he cleaned diesel and resold it across the border, the profit hidden under the guise of legitimate business concerns, and how he'd then put the cash into property, rightly considered a handsome investment that had been set to soar in value over the next ten or twenty years.

I'd understood, of course, that our business was illegal, but also that most of the people involved didn't consider it immoral. It was more like taking advantage of an unfair arrangement which the British government had foisted upon the Catholic underclass of Northern Ireland, namely, that a great bloody chunk of our homeland remained under British rule, carved up with an imaginary border.

The land had been raped once, and now we, the locals, the ones kept uneducated and poor, were clutching back some of the Queen's sterling by exploiting the gaping hole left in Ireland. I understood the nature of the business meant that occasionally, some young pups who snapped around Dad's ankles with pretensions to his throne had to be smacked down before they grew serious teeth. I even felt a sort of sympathy, and, buried deep down, a pride in what he did, and why.

Equally, as I grew older and saw the ever-more-sophisticated methods the law employed to combat smuggling, and the extremities to which Dad was driven in order to protect his turf, I knew I wanted no part of it.

I didn't like the sort of men Dad aligned himself with. I didn't like the self-righteousness, the anger, the gloating over money, the calculated violence, the flash cars, the showy women.

Gradually, I realised I didn't like my dad.

The crunch had come when he'd crashed into my room one night to excitedly explain some new tax dodge, and I'd turned to him and said, 'Do you mind? I'm trying to study history, not live off its legacy.' Yeah. Cold.

He'd never treated me the same way after that. Maybe we'd always been strangers, and it had taken one outburst to reveal it to both of us. History or not, I'd still gladly accepted a monthly allowance when I went to UCD, though. I told myself that I'd chosen earning an honest living over being a part of my dad's business empire.

The allowance would last as long as I was a student, and what I did after that was my own business. I was due to graduate next year with a degree in history, a part-time job in a bar, and no prospects.

Looking at the back of my dad's head, a roll of fat blubbering over the crisp white collar of his shirt, I wondered how much the old man could see of my future. It wasn't in either of our natures to make a big scene about my return home. What was so important that he had to drag me away from Duncan's wake?

We walked past the kids playing hopscotch in between cars parked at reckless angles. The estate had been designed to discourage groups of residents gathering for a common purpose, in case the proles turned to rioting. It hadn't worked. Our townland, Newry and Mourne, was famous for its home-grown army, and no part of it more so than Crossmaglen.

Dismal greenery, utilitarian housing, telegraph poles, back-to-back buildings, satellite dishes, porch ornamentation and yapping dogs. Was it worth it?

The cheap tarmac under our feet glistened in the afternoon sun. It was black and oily, the sort of mixture more often used to patch up road works, not cover entire pavements. It didn't take chalk very well. The ghosts of previous children's games loomed up out of the ground.

The corpse of a car was propped up on bricks in someone's front yard. Flakes of blue paint clung to the mottled carcass, its headlights smashed in, its windshield shattered, shards of glass clinging to the puckered rubber that held them in place. Two boys sped past on a motorbike, knees dirty, no helmets, the one behind clinging to the driver's stomach as he leant low over the handlebars, grinning his face off. Exhaust fumes lingered in the air like a petrochemical sneeze.

I wondered how Dad's diesel-smuggling business was doing.

We stopped at the edge of the estate.

A giant circle of burnt earth showed where a bonfire had recently been built, lit and spent. Tyres, tins, coils of wire, charred timber and lumps of melted plastic littered the scrubby wasteland overlooked by semi-detached council houses, people's homes.

Frank never did anything without a reason.

He was up to something.

'What do you think of this place?'

'Not much.'

'No. It's shite. A shite place to be from and a shite place to grow up. And who do you think put it here?'

'Is this going to be a rant against the Brits?'

Frank hacked up half a lung, and spat a gobbet of phlegm neatly into the centre of the circle of burnt earth.

'We did it. We built it, and we live here, and we're grateful. Grateful for living in this shite. We take what we get and we like it, like good little Catholics.'

A scabby crow inspected Frank's phlegm quizzically, turned its beady eyes towards us, and flapped off.

'Smart crow,' Frank said. 'A good Protestant crow. Won't take the first shite that comes its way.'

I loosened my tie and undid the top button of my shirt. The whiskey still burned in my stomach. It cast a warm glow over the otherwise unlovely surroundings, and I felt something dangerously close to nostalgia for dear old Crossmaglen. I didn't remember it as being all bad, but then, I'd had the benefit of my dad's money behind me. Frank had never had that comfort as a child, and he was reminding me that I'd turned my back on the greatest gift he'd had to offer me. The security that comes with cash, and a future.

'This is where I come from. This estate is what I've left

behind. Doing what I do is the only way someone like me could get out. Make a bit of money. I don't have your brains, you got them from your mother, thank God, but my old man gave me a good head for poker if nothing else. I know how to play the hand I'm dealt. I'm winning. Truth is though, business could be better.'

A faint breeze stirred the ashes of the bonfire, casting up a cloud of dust that danced in the air like black magic, and then fell lifeless to the ground again.

'Duncan's death might be sad. Sad for the family. From a business point of view . . .'

Frank's words tailed off into the breeze.

My throat was dry. I needed another drink.

'. . . you could say it's not the worst thing that might've happened. Understand?'

I nodded.

'Duncan was shooting his mouth off when he got too pissed, which was a lot. I had to have words with him over it. Who knows? He might've turned over a new leaf.'

We were enough alike for us both to know that if Duncan hadn't changed, something would've had to be done about him.

'Or he might have been persuaded,' I said.

'It doesn't matter now. What matters is, I can replace Duncan, in the long term. But in the short term, there's a problem.'

I knew where this was going. Still, I had to ask. It was part of the ritual that had begun with the tour of the estate, the talk about the business, the discussion of the temporary hole left behind by Duncan's death.

'Why are you telling me this?'

Frank turned to me solemnly.

I felt a bead of sweat trickle down my spine.

'If I said I had a small business proposal to put to you, I'd expect you to listen. Not to make up your mind on the spot, and not to tell me to shove it up my arse before you've had the good grace to listen. You with me?'

Bad idea, my brain said.

Bad idea to listen. Don't do it, don't do it . . .

The bigger part of me, the irrational, curious part, the part that remembered the awe with which people from home spoke of my dad in hushed tones, just wanted to hear what the old man had to say.

Just scratching an itch, I told my brain, *so shut up.*

I nodded once more.

'Duncan had a small job coming up. Just routine, but I can't use any of my other regulars for it right now. The long and the short of it is, I need a man to take a van to England. You don't need to know why. No one gets hurt. I don't do prozzies and I don't do weapons.'

'I know that.'

'Good. Now, you're a clean skin. You could drive this van over on the ferry. Only snag being, you're my son. Your name comes up, they know who you are. So we give you a different name. You'll have the right documents, they won't even glance at them twice. Worst-case scenario, you're detained, and I sort it out with one phone call. Never mind about that. If it goes according to plan, you sail to Wales, then drive the van to another place – I'll tell you where by phone once you're off the ferry – where the van's picked up by another man you've never met. Then you get a train to

London and fly home under your own name, after destroying the false documents and mobile I've given you. Got it?'

It sounded simple.

It *was* simple.

I pictured my crappy flat in Dublin, my part-time job keeping and sweeping the bar, the nights alone in front of the box, and the endless, grinding hours of a wage slave that lay ahead after I graduated.

'How much?'

Frank grinned.

'For you, one hundred grand.'

'Fuck off! That's a small fortune.'

'Keep your voice down.'

I looked around.

A mum turned her child away from us, walking quickly in the opposite direction.

I turned back to my dad.

'The job can't be worth that much. What's the catch?'

Frank's jowls wobbled with delight.

'Believe me, it's worth it. You're getting a family rate, plus it's short notice, plus it's a once-off. I know you wouldn't do it for any less.'

'How do you know that?'

'I know my own son. Think about it.' He slapped me on the back. 'I'll talk to you tomorrow, after the funeral.'

Frank left me leaning over the fence that marked the edge of the estate. Bile rose in my gullet. I heaved, puking neatly into no man's land, not entirely sure which part of the last half hour had prompted the emergency evacuation of my stomach.

Northern Ireland has changed. You don't watch your back every second. You don't expect to find soldiers in every ditch. You don't see lookout posts on every hill.

How many times had I lain in bed, listening to bullets erupt and bombs explode in the street? I can't remember.

Shootings and explosions had been a part of my youth, like school and football and television, things that just were. Maybe it was odd that I hadn't paid much attention to the civil war on my doorstep, but Northern Ireland in the Nineties was a strange place to grow up.

You had Saturday-morning TV, Top of the Pops, Woolworths, British schoolbooks and the Eleven Plus, but you never knew when a bomb might blow your living room windows in.

But I'd also known that Frank's smuggling business was dependent on there being a Northern Ireland. We needed British rule to exploit the holes in the border. We couldn't be on both sides at once. In my own mind, I'd always been sure that Frank's loyalties lay more with money than with a united Ireland, and that was partly why I'd grown uneasy about the money.

I thought about the acts of war I'd witnessed, back before the Muslims had become the terrorists.

The night I'd stayed over in Mike's house, when we were eight or nine. we'd been pushing each other's feet for control of the middle of the bed when a huge boom shook the house. We'd stopped kicking. We'd thought it was a bomb.

Then voices, loud English voices, filled our ears.

Mike's mum screamed.

Stamping feet.

'Go, go, go!'

The door burst open, torches, guns.

'Just kids.'

'Where is he?'

'Other bedroom.'

A blur of men in black, gleaming metal, radio static, the crackle of walkie-talkies, and Mike's granddad was dragged from his room, a frail old man in his pyjamas, blind and gummy and held up by the armpits, a gun in his chest, his face a sunken death mask.

'The children, for God's sake, let me get the children!'

'Hold her back.'

'Let her through.'

'Get the kids out.'

We were dragged out of bed, Mike crying, me speechless, trying to take it all in.

'Search the woman, get them out of the house.'

We were grabbed by the elbows and dragged outside.

I looked back over my shoulder at the door hanging off a splintered frame, as metal cracked on bone inside the house, stone-faced soldiers surrounding us, guns raised.

One of the neighbours had taken us in, but only after the Brits had dragged Mike's granddad off to the army base.

There'd never been an opportunity for Mike's family to complain. The cops had said they were acting on information received, that the old man in the house was a terrorist, that if the whole family weren't terrorists then they knew people who were, that this was the price ordinary citizens paid for freedom. The cops had never got anything out of the old man or anyone else in Mike's family.

Another time, I'd had to pick up Scarlett after school. I was two years older than her, in my second year at the big school, and the grown-ups were visiting somebody in hospital. I'd sauntered through the primary-school gates just as streams of kids had poured from the double doors. I was thinking how small they looked, how funny it was to see these little people so excited by running out into the sun at three o' clock in the day, keeping an eye out for Scarlett's blonde plaits amidst all the dark heads. Then one kid had stopped, pointed, and we turned as one to see the sniper perched at the school railings, taking cover behind a convenient tree, snapping the last piece of his gun into place.

Did a hush fall upon the schoolyard, or was that only in my imagination?

A tug at my sleeve.

I swept Scarlett up into my arms.

I turned towards the gunman, so that Scarlett was looking in the opposite direction, over my shoulder.

I saw him fire one, two, three shots in rapid succession somewhere into the heart of town, where the soldiers in camouflage stood ripe and green against the slabs of concrete.

Mums and dads clutched their children. Kids stood dead still and stared, or turned to each other, hands over mouths, eyes wide. A clamour to get back inside the school – the soldiers might open fire in our direction – while the sniper coolly packed up and walked away without a backwards glance.

Crossmaglen had changed too.

I'd read about the lookout post being torn down, but seeing the square without the looming, metal monstrosity with a winking black window on top was still a shock.

When I'd walked past the lookout post back in the day,

I'd always imagined a couple of soldiers hefting their guns and gazing down upon the town through the crosshairs of their weapons.

The square's statues, its community centre, its erratic take on parking were all intact. There was now a posh hotel in the middle of the determinedly not posh pubs. There was an optician's which proudly declared itself part funded by a project for the regeneration of South Armagh. Well, there'd never been anything wrong with our snipers' eyesight.

A gleaming supermarket sat opposite the chapel, the two buildings staring each other down from across the road like cowboys in a duel with their hands on their holsters. The chapel, perched as it was on its hill, looked down its nose at the traffic buzzing by, knowing full well that those driving past would one day be laid to rest beneath a stone slab at its feet. The names on our headstones had not changed for centuries.

The GAA pitch was still there, despite nestling flank by flank with the army base. I remembered helicopters swooping as low to the ground as they could without coming in to land, the coach yelling at us to drop to the ground as the helicopters sliced through the air just above our bad haircuts, his voice almost drowned out by the drone of the propellers.

I turned my back to the fence, slid down on my hunkers, and wiped my mouth with the back of my hand.

I felt a whole lot better.

I feel like I can predict the trajectory of most of my friends' lives, bar the whims of extreme luck, good or bad. Since I'd left home, I'd had no dramatic changes of fortune. The usual. Friends and lovers came and went. Job opportunities presented themselves, or didn't, were taken, or closed off. Money, sex, and drink were in short supply, or sudden plenty. I could see my gradual drift downwards, towards the level of the losers I served in the bar. Why should my life story be any less predictable than other people's?

There was the ditch where a classmate had crashed his car and bled to death. There was the handball alley where the sluttier girls might let you finger them on a Saturday night. There was the secondary school I hadn't gone to, in fact, had known from no age I'd never attend. It seemed as if I'd always known the local high school was for the kids who'd never leave town. It hadn't been said, but I knew it.

You picked up these things by a sort of osmosis, in the space in between nods and glances, through the offhand remarks you never forgot, by how your parents spoke and behaved, especially when you were an only child. Siblings were more blunt about how the world worked. The rougher kids I'd met at school, the ones I kept my distance from, were my first clue that all people were not equal, despite what the priest said at Mass. Just look around. The drooling retard wasn't equal. The boy in hand-me-down clothes wasn't equal. The shuffling drunks at the back of the church weren't the equal of the scrubbed and polished families in the front rows every Sunday.

I hadn't set foot in a church in years, but now there was no way to avoid it.

Still, there might be some perks to being back home.

I could take advantage of that inequality.

One hundred grand.

There was no doubt.

I was tempted.

3

Fight

'See? That went quite well,' Dolores said, reversing over a carelessly abandoned child's doll on the way out of the estate. It squeaked once in protest and fell silent. Several mourners waved from Aunty Kate's front porch.

'You shouldn't have drank so much, though. That old baggage Fidelma will be telling the whole country you're about to go the same way as your poor cousin Duncan.'

'I'm upset. Am I allowed to be upset?'

'Of course. You're supposed to be upset. Just don't over-do it in front of other people, it's a sign of weakness. Look at you. You're a mess. Let's get you a new suit.'

'Got any cigarettes?'

'Of course I do, and they're genuine bought and paid for, in case you're wondering.' Dolores shook loose a cigarette, lit up, and leaned back, as we zipped through the country roads as smoothly as a motorway.

'None of your smuggled brands for me, thanks. And you shouldn't smoke, by the way. Awful habit, and so expensive.'

'What's your excuse?'

'I'll buy a new pair of lungs when I've worn these out. You'll never be able to afford it, not with an arts degree.'

The smooth-talking radio host invited listeners to phone in and air their grievances about marriage equality, the role of the Church in state education, the meaning of the local election results and their ramifications for the Northern Irish peace process, the ongoing investigations into police collusion and corruption during the Troubles, the likelihood of the families of the disappeared ever having the bodies of their loved ones recovered, or parents opposed to childhood vaccinations.

I hadn't heard the local news in three years, but nothing had changed. Dolores turned off the radio.

'I can't stand the sound of real people talking. They're so embarrassing.'

The drive was soothing after that.

I was surprised by how much my dad hadn't changed. I could still picture him all those years ago, doing deals behind half-closed doors with loud, fat men, catching a glimpse of a handshake or a headshake as Dolores swept through the door with bottles of whiskey.

The mysteries of the adult world, as seen through banisters, and always with my dad at the centre, the one holding court, the one they all listened to. I'd been proud of him, but afraid of him too, just like all his loud, fat friends had seemed to be.

My parents confused me. They loved me, they looked after me, they knew everything, and just when I'd realised that not everyone was as lucky as I was, I'd begun to see their flaws.

If parents were the moral compass of youth, no wonder I'd been confused.

I thought about all the bad things that had happened in individual moments, strung together over the course of years. Years of seeing my hometown on the telly, each side blaming the other for the latest atrocity. Helicopters landing in the fields behind my home.

Retaliation, random shootings, planned bomb attacks. An endless barrage of tit-for-tat violence interspersed with boring roadblocks. The arrest, assault, and, usually, the release of people I knew. The impassable resentment of one people for another.

In all likelihood, Crossmaglen probably hadn't been as bad as some other parts of the North. Almost all of us were Catholic, so you didn't have the seething bitterness between neighbours that you did in Belfast – not on religious grounds, anyway. The only Protestants in town were a few good neighbours, who were liked and accepted as such, and the ones who lived in the barracks, who were distrusted, despised and hated for it.

By and large, they were also the ones who got murdered, until an innocent bystander got shot, or a joyriding kid was killed on the assumption he was armed. I wondered who was able to keep track of where colonialism ended and terrorism began. But then, plenty of people kept score of who had been killed on either side, although they didn't necessarily agree on who started it.

In my mind, the Troubles were hopelessly conflated with religious education.

Received wisdom says the war was sectarian, fought along a religious divide, but now, with the benefit of hindsight, it looked to me largely like a class war between the haves and the have-nots.

What had religion got to with anything, except the various flavours of lessons at school? My own religious education was still there, imprinted on my memory. We'd learned reams of doggerel, and that sort of early indoctrination never leaves you. I could reel off the Ten Commandments, the names of the Apostles, the Joyful, Glorious, and Sorrowful Mysteries, prayers in both English and Irish. I could reel them off and not think twice about the words I was saying, or the meaning behind them.

They were rhythmic gibberish, learned by rote, and all for the sake of a ceremony.

Catholicism loves a ceremony. An awful lot of time and energy at school had gone into learning your lines for Communion and Confirmation. That was fine with most of the kids. Anything that wasn't spelling and maths was a welcome relief. You didn't have exams in religion, you just had to show up and say a few words, and everyone thought you were great.

The boring part for most of the boys was getting kitted out in a new suit. The girls talked about their dresses endlessly, how they were wearing their hair, whether or not they were allowed to wear makeup, but for the boys, it was just another dull day down the shops while your mum fussed over whether you should have one row of buttons or two, a tie or a dicky bow, something fancy that you'd only wear once, or something classic that you'd wear again.

Religion came down to a string of rehearsals for pageant after pageant, ending with you in your Sunday best and a silk-lined box.

I stood in front of the mirror in the gents' outfitters in Newry. The shirt and tie I'd chosen were the same colour as our old school uniform. I sank down in the corner of the changing room, hugged my knees, and wept silently. I sat there alone until the sobbing subsided, then emerged, pink-faced and puffy-eyed, to pay for my new clothes.

To her credit, Dolores pretended that she couldn't tell I'd been crying.

We had lunch in a chain-store café. Dolores systematically rubbed crumbs from her fingers and dabbed minute morsels of food from her lips while watching the locals with barely disguised scorn.

An obese mother of twins waddled by, her offspring sucking on bottles of cola in their pushchair. She berated her skinny boyfriend with a harsh tongue.

'Those children,' Dolores declared, 'would be better off drowned at birth than weaned on Coca-Cola and forced to listen to that nagging lump all day.'

To our left, a middle-aged man explained to his confused mother that the tea in front of her was, in fact, her own.

'But you ordered it, mother.'

'I never.'

'You did, remember mother, you ordered it just now from the nice girl at the till.'

A passing waitress smiled sympathetically.

'I never. I don't like coffee.'

'It's tea, mother, drink up your nice tea.'

'Oh, put her in a home,' Dolores said loudly, 'and stop parading your milksop martyrdom to people forced to interact with you in public.'

The waitress bit her lip and stifled a snort.

The middle-aged man looked scandalised, turned red, then leapt squealing from his seat as his mother tipped her pot of scalding tea onto his lap.

'I told you I don't like coffee,' the old woman said smugly.

On our way back to the car park, we passed a boy collecting for charity.

'What's the charity, dear?'

'T-Trócaire, madam, to h-help developing nations in Africa.'

'Well,' Dolores said, dropping a two-pound coin into the charity box, 'just remember, if you help yourself to a few pounds from the box, you're helping delay the Africans' inevitable descent into sedentary obesity, heart disease and cancer. Being hungry gives poor people a sense of purpose, dear.'

We left the earnest youth staring after us with his mouth hanging open.

Back home, I managed a couple of hours' kip on the sofa. I woke up, ate the dinner Dolores had prepared for me and all the wake-goers, texted Martin, and got ready to go out.

'You don't want to be hungover for the funeral tomorrow.'

'I'll be fine. I just want to see what's happening in town, catch up with Martin, get a feel for the old place. It's been ages since I was out at home.'

'It might look different, but the people are the same.'

'I won't stay out all night, and I won't be drinking and driving.'

'I'll give you a lift.'

'No, don't bother. I'd rather walk, clear my head. You've got enough to do.'

'Well, I suppose one drink won't kill you. Although look what it did to Duncan.'

I took the spare key for the front door, and kissed Dolores on the cheek.

'Be careful.'

'I will.'

All mothers think their children need to be reminded to look both ways before they cross the road. First you need it, then you resent it, then you accept it.

I set my shoulders against the chill embrace of the air and headed for town. I waved on a couple of cars when they slowed down to offer a lift. The cool calmness of descending night helped clear my fuzzy mind. A slight breeze ruffled my hair. The shape of the world around me took on a smooth, marble nothingness. Electric lights glowed and televisions hummed behind drawn curtains. The evening sky was a milky mauve.

The land stretched green and brown in every direction, dotted with dwellings, either new and solid, or old and covered with ivy and moss, falling apart as trees flourished amidst the hobbled piles of stone.

It was only a couple of miles' walk, a distance you'd cover in the city without noticing the time slide by, as there'd always be some distraction.

Here, in the countryside, time moved slowly. I was aware of every footstep, trudge, trudge, trudge, one foot in front of the other, crushing grass and twigs in the ditch, kicking stones and bottles over hedges, just for fun. I kept an ear out for cars or vans, either of which might speed along the winding road, thinking nothing of turning a corner on the twist of a ditch.

Not many people walked these roads, especially at night. A sports car zoomed in and zipped out of earshot. Straggling tractors, bound for home after a long day on the farm, would be too slow to mow you down. Cattle lowed in the distance.

As long as joyriders didn't smoosh into me out of nowhere, the worst I'd have to navigate was cow shit.

The army base was still vast, despite the removal of the lookout post. What was the point of it?

Arguably, it had bred more violence by being there, an obvious target for those who wanted to crush the British occupation of Ireland. I could see that not having an army presence on a notoriously Republican part of the border would be inviting an arms route into the country, but had the tactics of intimidation been counterproductive?

Had they given a very real enemy to people who would otherwise have grown up with only stories to tell us about the evils done by Englishmen in the name of keeping the Irish in our place?

The idea that they were there to keep peace between two communities never made sense in Catholic Crossmaglen. Maybe it had seemed necessary. Maybe it had been a huge error in judgement.

Either way, with sectarian violence now officially denounced by both sides, only flaring up occasionally amongst dissatisfied dissident groups who were largely kept in check by other gangs, it was time to dismantle the sprawling tin can that housed the army.

The hand-painted billboards which had sloganeered the fight against the Brits were a dying art now, belonging to a time when I'd slept through bomb attacks, or woken up to spurts of gunfire, mentally shrugged, and gone back to sleep. There were still bullet holes in the road signs pointing in and out of town. I remembered women in balaclavas marching down these roads every Easter, under Republican banners. It all seemed so long ago.

There'd only been one time I'd really tasted the blood in the air, the time I'd first met Martin.

My phone buzzed in my pocket. It was Martin, texting back to say he'd meet me down the pub. We both knew which pub he meant. It had been our pub when we hung out more, not too dimly lit, not too full of alcos propping up the bar with their personal problems, not too depressing.

Warmth hit me as I pushed open the door.

I relaxed.

I ordered a pint of Guinness from a kid at the bar whom I didn't recognise, but who had the same ears and chin as a guy I'd known at school. Probably a brother, or a cousin.

I scanned the room as my Guinness settled. I recognised one or two faces, took a sup of my pint, and caught my own gaze in the mirror behind the bar. My face was pale, my eyes ringed with purple smudges. I rasped fingernails over my stubble and searched for a seat.

'Jay O'Reilly!'

'Martin Furey!'

Lamplight caught the fire in Martin's hair.

He put his head to one side and grinned.

He was five foot tall and change, buff, youthful.

'Long time no see. You must be home for your cousin's funeral. It's all over the news. Local man, links with organised crime. All that shit. Sorry for your trouble, man.'

'Thanks, Martin.'

We shook hands solemnly. Martin had been a friendly kid, entirely without guile, who'd said exactly what he'd thought at any time. He'd never fit in, and I liked him all the more for it. He'd been born after his mother ran off with a gypsy, the product of a short, brutal marriage, which everyone had expected to fail.

Everyone had been right.

Gypsies didn't stay married to settled women, we'd all known that. Martin had grown up without a dad, which some people blamed for his sissiness.

There were plenty of other sissies who had dads – rough dads, tough dads, boring dads, drunken dads, normal dads – but it was Martin who'd borne the brunt of the teasing.

'You're down in Dublin, aren't you?'

'Yeah, I am. Been there for three years. What are you up to?'

'Ah, nothing much,' Martin said, slurping beer. 'I was doing some work on the building sites, that was good money for a while, but the arse has fallen out of it. You know yourself.'

'Yeah, of course. That's tough.'

'Any women on the scene? You married?'

'No, no women, no kids. Thank God, ha.'

'Touch wood,' Martin said, suiting the action to the word by means of the nearest barstool, 'it'll stay that way for a few years yet. But come here to me, you must be loaded these days, huh?'

'Loaded? No. I'm a student. I work part-time in a bar, but I'm far from loaded.'

Martin couldn't conceal his surprise. His eyes grew wide.

'But man,' he said, lowering his voice, 'what about all the other work you're doing?'

'What other work?'

'For your dad.'

'But I don't work for my dad.'

Martin's eyebrows disappeared into his fringe.

'Seriously, man, I don't. Never have. That's kind of why I left home for Dublin.'

'Well fair play to you for sticking to your guns,' Martin said with a shake of his head, 'but you must be stone mad.'

'Why?'

'Why? Why? Man, you're the luckiest son of a bitch who's standing here in this pub – no offence to Dolores. Your dad's loaded, the cops can't touch him, you've a job for life if you want it. You should be raking it in. I tell you, if I had your life . . .'

But what it was that Martin would do if by some miracle we were to trade places, I'd never find out.

A bottle smashed on a table top.

A girl screamed.

A fist landed in a man's stomach.

A young lad was on the floor.

People drew back.

Martin spun around with his mouth wide open.

Two lads, short and rough, were at the centre of the scrap. One jumped up on a table and booted a man in the face. The other punched a guy a good head taller, but two stone lighter. The tall guy went down. The boot went in. The other young lad struggled up off the floor. Blood streamed from his nose. A couple dragged him back.

The first short, rough guy – they looked like brothers – had hopped off the table, taunting bystanders. He swung around to help kick the man who was still down.

Two of the bar staff fell upon the fighters, dragging them off.

Broken glass glistened amid splatters of blood.

Men yelled, women wailed, camera phones snapped.

The two lads were dragged outside, whooping like lunatics.

The crowd closed in around the injured men.

Someone shouted, 'Give them space!'

A glamorous blonde looked with disgust at the blood-stains spattered over the thin white fabric stretched across her tits. A mop appeared to clean up the mess. A man bought pints for the guys still bleeding from their head wounds. They drank through bloody lips, tenderly feeling their jaws, their bodies.

'Jesus, man, I wouldn't want to be those two boys tomorrow,' Martin said.

'Few stitches, they'll be grand.'

'No, I mean the McGinley brothers. You know them, right?'

I shook my head.

Martin laughed.

'Where've you been? Those two cocks are the sons of Ian McGinley.'

'Who?'

Some of the eyes at the bar were turned warily in my direction.

'Ian McGinley! Ian McGinley! Muck McGinley, your dad's biggest fucking rival in these parts!'

'Never heard of him.'

'Your dad won't be happy when he hears about this. Don't tell me you don't know Shane and Mark?'

'Nope.'

'They work for your dad. Now do you get it?'

'I do. Maybe we should fuck off.'

I skulled my pint.

'Yeah, come on.'

Outside, there was no sign of the brothers McGinley.

My breath hovered like a foggy cloud in the cool, damp air, and was gone.

Worst. Pint. Ever.

4

Holding Hands

Town was almost deserted, like it would've been after a bomb attack years ago. Two shadowy figures entwined by the cash machine broke their embrace and returned to their car, which swallowed them whole and sped off.

There was a Chinese restaurant where there'd once been a chippy, and its front window had been shattered with a brick. A man emerged from the restaurant with a large piece of cardboard, and stoically set about tacking it in place over the broken window. It looked as if he'd done it before.

The litter whipped half-heartedly around the gutters. Stale horse manure from that week's street fair was trodden into the street. Torn posters tacked on to telephone poles fluttered around in useless tatters.

I was buzzing a little from drinking my pint too quickly. As usual, drinking helped mask the squalor. The alcohol leant an almost glamorous sheen to the otherwise tawdry surroundings.

'You know I'm a fag now, right?'

'No, I didn't,' I lied. I'd always known.

'Don't worry, I'm not going to jump your bones. Half-gypsy, all homo, and fucking ginger as well. Don't know how I made it this far in one piece. You look like you're going to puke.'

'Not coz you're gay. Just coz I drank that pint too quickly.'

The buildings were mute and impassive in the grainy glow of the neon-lit night. We walked as far as the army barracks, less potent now without its totemic lookout post, but still there, sprawling like a belligerent drunkard, refusing to get up and go home.

I remembered the town before its rejuvenation, a pile of rubble and crap, unkempt and ugly, like any other war zone you'd see on the telly. Broken bricks and bits of metal had once been strewn around like battle scars, but that had all been cleaned up.

Now there were shrubs and trees, bins and benches, parking spaces to facilitate local businesses, and statues symbolising hope in the face of adversity, all clustered around the barracks, which stared back blankly from its hill.

The barracks is an army base protected by a fence made of corrugated metal. It sprawls over a strategic piece of land which straddles the highest point of the square and the football pitch, taking over the swathe of land in between, like a fat-arsed bastard hitching a ride on public transport, squeezed into the best seats between two paying customers.

The land had belonged to locals, until the British army took it over. Now they've got a barracks in their backyard. I used to go to playschool in one of the terraced houses on the street. Every fine day we'd eat our lunch in the yard, under the shadow of the barracks.

It was in the ghost of this place that Martin and I had first met.

It had been a Saturday, two weeks before Martin's Confirmation. He told me that his head had been full of prayers and rituals, what to say, when to kneel, and when to walk to the top of the church, stand before the altar, and, with his dad's hand on his shoulder and the priest's finger-tips on his forehead, receive the Holy Spirit into his soul.

I remember Martin carefully balancing the white plastic bag full of shopping on the handlebar of his bike. I remember him wobbling slightly as he pedalled off from the kerb, the weight of the bag pulling him into the road. I remember the bright afternoon blue of the sky. A bunch of lads were playing football by the roadside, kicking a crappy old leather thing around on a makeshift pitch, with goalposts marked by their rolled-up jumpers.

One of them called Martin a queer, which was even worse than being called a gyppo. Martin ignored him. The heel broke on a woman's shoe, and she swore, bending over to take it from her foot. A man with a moustache opened his car door, looked over his shoulder, and froze as a lorry pulled up to the barracks.

The lorry roared.

Martin fell from his bike.

Shopping spilled across the road.

Boom.

An enormous rumble. A dirty great crunch. Tattered tarpaulin flew in every direction. The smell of metal and diesel, and something else I couldn't place.

Martin stood up.

'Get down!'

I ran across the road, grabbing him from behind, dragging him down to his knees. I felt the warm ooze of blood seep from beneath my skin, puddling in the tarmac.

The lorry shuddered, flinging something over the high

corrugated metal shanks of the army base, exploding on impact on the other side.

Boom.

Metal rattled. Chunks of bricks and bodies rained down. I held Martin tighter, whispering, 'Keep still, don't move, keep still,' over and over as the first stutters of gunfire splattered bullets all around. The bunch of lads who had been playing football whimpered. A stray bullet had burst the leather ball. It lay gutted in the middle of the road.

The lorry groaned and pulled off, drawing gunfire away from all the people lying in the road. I found Martin's hand with my own. Our fingers intertwined. My breath was on his neck, my legs wrapped around his legs, holding hands.

Martin's thumb slid against mine.

The shooting ceased.

That was it. The stench of death rising through the clouds of smoke.

'It's OK. It's over.'

I sensed that Martin did not want me to let go of his hand.

'You're bleeding,' he said.

'I've just cut my knee, that's all.'

'What's your name?'

'James.'

'That's a good name.'

'Call me Jay.'

Two weeks later Martin chose James as his Confirmation name. We'd become friends.

The reek of petrol and sweat.

Blood on the pavement.

A boy's hand in mine.

We both stared up at the vast expanse of concrete and metal which loomed over us.

'The statue's kind of ugly, isn't it?' Martin said, recalling me to the present.

'Important, though. Freedom fighters and all that.'

'Yeah.'

We walked on.

Pale light twinkled on a crumpled Coke tin. The shiny foil of a torn-open crisp bag smeared a shrub in silver. The neon street lamp teased out hints of orange in the dull brown gleam of a beer bottle discarded in the gutter.

Behind us, a drunken man stumbled from a pub, singing with loud, lusty booziness.

'So, was the funeral the only reason you came home?'

'I was curious to see my dad again.'

'You hadn't seen him since you left home?'

'Nope.'

'Wow. What was that like?'

'I saw him today. It was like nothing had really changed. Like the three years I'd been gone had happened to someone else. Like I was right back where I belonged.'

'Maybe you do.'

'I hope not.'

'Why?'

We were almost at Martin's estate, but stopped instinctively at the sound of raised voices ahead.

'You stole my feed!'

'I never stole your feed!'

'You did, you snatched it, right there from under my nose

when I went for a piss round the corner from the Chinese.'

'Did you piss on your feed?'

'What?'

'Did you piss on your feed?'

'No.'

'Well unless you piss backwards, it wasn't under your nose, was it?'

Lads hooted with laughter.

'I left it in the Chinese and you lifted it when my back was turned.'

'I did no such thing.'

'You did.'

'So where is it?'

'You scoffed it already, you hungry bastard, you scoffed it on the way up the road before I clocked on to what you were doing, and followed you up here.'

'Aye, well you'll not follow me up my road.'

'I will follow you up your road.'

'You will not, you unmannerly bastard, follow me up none of my road.'

'If you can't gimme back my feed, you'd better pay for it.'

'I never took your feed.'

'You're making a show of me.'

'You're making a show of yourself.'

'If you don't gimme back my feed, I'll flatten you.'

'Might as well keep walking,' I said.

'Want to cross the road?'

'Yeah.'

'Get your jacket off and fight me like a man. We'll settle

this right now. You'll not follow me up my road!'

'I'm ready for you.'

'Two fights in one night,' I said, as we passed the lads brawling on the lip of their estate, jackets flung to the ground, their mates dancing around and yelling encouragement.

'Stupid wee bollixes.' said Martin

The two lads were locked together, rolling on dead grass under sick yellow light.

'Get up on him!'

'Pin his arms down!'

'For fuck sake, are you gonna fight him, or are you gonna make love to him?'

'Hot,' Martin said.

'You're almost home.'

'Yeah. That's our house, the one with no wall around the front yard. My mum tore down the hedge just before Dad left, and she never got around to replacing it.'

'Everyone used to have hedges on this road.'

'I suppose walls are handier. You can sit on them.'

Martin put the heel of his hands on his neighbour's wall, and hauled himself up on it. His feet swung above the pavement. I leaned against the wall beside him.

'So, you never said why you hoped you didn't belong here.'

'It's complicated.'

'I bet I can make it simple for you.'

The drunk was still singing. The lads were still fighting. Lights died one by one behind windows.

'I felt that, if I came home, my dad might make me an offer of some sort. Call a truce. I do something for him, he puts me on my feet, financially.'

'And did he?'

'He did.'

'And what did you say?'

'Nothing, yet. But I'm only home for a few days, so I have to decide soon.'

We sat in the dark on the last road out of the United Kingdom of Great Britain and Northern Ireland, before you reached the Republic of Ireland.

'Look at this stupid made-up country,' Martin said. 'Who wants it? No one. To the Brits, we're just a nuisance, taking their benefits and whinging about a past they don't even learn about at school. The Irish think we're all a bunch of God-bothering murderers, and they can't afford to pay for us to be a part of their country anyway. And we're stuck in the middle with only ourselves for company, a hundred years behind the rest of Europe, racist and homophobic and stupidly devout because we've nothing else to talk about. Churches and shopping centres, that's all we've got. We're a race of bastards, stuck between two parents, and neither of them want us. I know what that's like. You act up just to get attention from either of them, and they both end up hating you more.'

'Harsh.'

'True.'

'Right, but what about me?'

'Look, it's like this. You can't help being part of your family. It's who you are. You might've turned your back on them for a while, but you can't avoid them forever. So what if you don't like what your dad does for a living? Lots of people hate their family business, but it's money. You could say you started off with the triple disadvantage of being from here, having a smuggler for a dad, and having enough brains to want to get out. Big deal. You've got options. I bet most people round here think you're lucky as hell.'

'And what do you think?'

'I think you should do what's best for Jay O'Reilly. If no one gets hurt, what's the harm?'

Martin slipped off the wall and punched me on the shoulder.

'Good to see you again. Hopefully I'll see you before you go back to Dublin.'

'Thanks. Night.'

Martin walked through the non-existent wall of their front yard, and was home. I stood up straight and squared my shoulders.

The drunk limped past the lads on their estate, his voice warbling thinly through the night air. The lads chortled and guffawed and slung insults at each other's backs, a sure sign that they were all on friendly terms again, and would enjoy recounting their own highly coloured versions of the night's events the next morning.

In idle moments with a spliff in hand, I'd come to imagine life after death as a vast cinema, where the film only started once every human being had died. Everyone sat in order of their death. You might be sat beside a four-year-old African child on one hand and an octogenarian Asian on the other. You waited for what seemed like forever, and then the film began – records of every moment of every human life ever lived, from birth to death.

It would begin with primitive humans scrabbling out an existence on the hot, unforgiving terrain that had borne them, and ran through aeons of evolution, development, the rise and fall of civilisations, religions, countries, love, fear, jealousy, loneliness, power, lust, hunger, misery, joy, hope, whatever, every moment, every emotion, every person, unimportant in their own lifetime or otherwise, whether they had breathed for only moments, or lived for decades.

There'd be no need for subtitles, as you'd learn every language as it came into being. There'd be repetition, of course, as lives touched other lives – but then, there would be private moments too, the hours spent sleeping, or doing nothing, or doing shameful things silently, alone, and, by the time you'd seen the first billion or so lives, you became immune to bodily functions, ill health, deformity, accidents, sex of any kind, abuse, depravity.

By the time it came to your turn, hundreds of thousands of years into human existence, you'd be amazed at how much you'd forgotten of your own humble beginnings, although everything that had come before had warned you that life is lived largely in forgotten moments.

You would remember your humdrum childhood as it unfolded once again before your eyes, and you'd forget to be ashamed of all the stupid, ugly things you'd ever done. Instead, you'd marvel at the simple life you'd lost, like everyone else, because there we all were, seeing our lives for what they really were – brief, some of them; dreary, a lot of them; wasted, too many of them; horrific, quite a few of them; exceptional, hardly any of them; oddly shot with moments of beauty, all of them.

And after every story that had ever existed had been told? That's where my imagination failed me.

'Don't play football with him,' one of the lads said. 'You don't know what he'd do to you in the showers after. He felt up Tommy's arse in his bedroom.'

'I never.'

'And he felt up Quinn's arse as well, he told me himself, after school one day. Don't go near him.'

'I didn't.'

'You did, you roly-poly faggot. Keep your fat hands off my bum. I'm telling your ma, and I'm telling Quinn's ma, and she's tougher than your old man, and you're gonna get a beating you won't forget, you smelly queer.'

'Kiss my arse.'

'You'd love that, wouldn't you?'

The alleged molester got a dig on the ribs, dug back, and the tussle continued.

The drunk man, bent double, stumbled into the arms of a drunk woman.

They flailed together, gabbling something in each other ears. The lads quit tussling and pointed at them, laughing. He fished a bottle out of his pocket, and her eyes rolled in their sockets, searching for something neither of them could see.

'Won't you open the bottle for him?' she wailed. 'He's only looking for you to open the bottle.'

They paused mid-reel beneath a lamp post. If the man was fifty, the woman could've been his mother. Crusted saliva flecked the cracks of her lips. She thrust a grasping claw in the lads' direction, her bloated face quivering in indignation.

'He can't open the bleeding bottle, couldn't you do that for him?'

'How the fuck am I meant to do that?'

'Why can't you, you miserable cunt?'

'Gimme the bottle then.'

One lad grabbed the bottle and smashed it against the lamp post. The other lads cheered. The drunk man and woman fell to the ground wailing, pressing their lips to the shards of glass that glistered on the street, as their alcohol evaporated into the night air.

'Go fuck yourselves, you pack of cunts.'

There was nothing more for me here.

In the morning, I'd tell Dad the job was mine.

5

Birds and Flowers

I woke up to the sound of birds chirruping on the windowsill. I've never liked the little bastards. They are the dinosaurs who survived. I don't trust them.

I yawned, stretched, and scratched my balls. I drew back the curtains. One of the little brown birds on the windowsill flew off into the buttery glow of the morning sunrise. The other put its head to one side, bobbed, and looked at me with tiny, shiny eyes.

'Scram!'

It was gone.

Downstairs, Dolores floated between the living room and kitchen, carrying by turns a fresh pot of tea, flowers, and ribbon.

'I'm making bouquets for the grave. Help yourself to some tea, and whatever you want for breakfast. You can smoke over the sink if you like, but open the window.'

I poured a cuppa, lit up, and stared into the garden. A black cat stalked through the grass. I smoked an entire cigarette without tasting it.

Dolores kept talking.

'The funeral's at half eleven. As well as getting the flowers ready and making sure your Aunty Anne and Aunty Nelly put some money towards the service – you know what they're like, mean as Protestants – I'm organising the readings. I thought it would be nice if you would do one? They're all chosen from a list, so you don't have to talk about your feelings or any of that nonsense.'

'Sure.'

'Good. Now, can you do me a favour, and drop off some flowers at Scarlett's house while I drive into town for some last-minute bits and pieces?'

'No problem.'

'Now, what else was there?'

Dolores stood still in the middle of the kitchen, a bouquet of lilies tied with white ribbon in her hand. The flowers looked voluptuous and lovely against the black satin sheen of her mourning, but I prefer decaying flowers – the brown, creeping tinge on the edge of a rose petal, the crisp, dry feel of an autumn leaf, the fetid, sick smell of blossoms on the turn.

'Yes, that's it. We noticed you were home early last night. We were expecting you to crawl home at all hours. Didn't you have a good time?'

'I only stayed for the one.'

'Oh, that's a shame. How come?'

'The McGinley brothers started a fight.'

'With you?'

'No, two of Dad's men. It was over in seconds, but I didn't want to hang around.'

'Oh, don't worry about that. Your father has that little problem under control. Come on, I'll give you a lift as far as Scarlett's estate. You know what these places are like. Muddly. I've written down some directions.'

Ten minutes later, I hopped out of the car and waved as Dolores sped off to the shops. I had to take a confusing number of turns through the jungle of houses in Scarlett's estate. Luckily, Dolores's directions were to the point. It felt a bit strange, carrying an elaborate bouquet of mourning flowers through the maze of council houses.

Each of the houses was built to the same model, although most people had taken pains to individualise their homes. Some had built porches with sliding doors protecting the homestead. Some had installed matching gates, light fixtures and summer seats. A few had well-tended yards with bushes, shrubs or trees.

It was a cosier estate than Aunty Kate's.

Scarlett's house had a red-brick wall and a white wooden garden gate. Two flower pots flanked the front door, spilling over with trailing tendrils, and embedded with small, soft pansies, brightly coloured with black eyes.

I pressed the buzzer. There was no sound from inside the house.

A plane scored a thin vapour trail in the sky. Escape was just a plane ticket away, if you had enough money for a ticket, and a plan to cover your tracks.

But how could you ever disappear completely, without giving up your identity, your friends, your social media, the job and the photos and the online library of music, books and film which made you a person?

I pressed the buzzer again.

Footsteps, and the door opened tentatively to reveal half of Scarlett's face.

'Special delivery,' I said, thrusting the flowers into her face.

Scarlett's hand fluttered to her mouth. Her hair had fallen over one eye.

'Can I come in?'

'Of course. Sorry, Jay. I'm a bit behind today . . .'

'That's cool. I don't usually get out of bed 'til the afternoon. Hope I didn't wake you up?'

Scarlett unchained the door, and opened it with a smile that seemed forced.

'Oh, they're beautiful. Thank you. No, no, I've been up . . .'

Inside the house, a baby squawled.

'Come in and meet Alison. You haven't seen her, have you?'

'I've seen photos.'

'We're having a bad day. She won't eat her yummy baby food.'

Scarlett took the flowers from me and let me follow her indoors.

Her home was not as bright and cheerful as I'd expected it to be. A pervasive smell of baby things, like nappies, powder, and plastic, hung over everything. A mishmash of shoes and clothes had been tossed under the stairs. The kitchen door was open, revealing dishes piled high in the sink, coffee rings on the small dining table, utensils and cutlery dotted on every surface.

Alison was in a walker in the living room, watching television with the sound turned off. She bounced up and down, mimicking the cartoon characters bouncing around on screen. Popular culture gets you when you're young, and soon you can't imagine leaving it all behind.

'Say hello to Uncle Jay.'

The child spun round with a smile. She was blonde and pretty, like her mother.

'Hello Alison.'

Alison shook her rattle, and turned back to her cartoon.

'She's beautiful. So is the daddy . . . ?'

'The guy I'm engaged to? Of course he is.'

'Sorry, that came out all wrong.'

'Oh, it's fine,' she said, although it clearly wasn't.

She absent-mindedly ran her fingers through her hair, sweeping back the locks that covered her eye. She wasn't wearing any make-up. A bruise covered the naked flesh around her left eye, as dark as the eyes of the pansies on her doorstep. She caught me staring, and blushed.

'I'll put these in water.'

'Scarlett—'

'It's none of your business, Jay.'

Alison began to cry.

We stood frozen for a second, her face red and angry. Then I took the flowers from her, she picked up Alison, and I went to the kitchen. My heart was beating much too fast. I found a dusty vase, rinsed it, filled it with water, and placed the flowers in it. I brought them back to the living room. The baby had stopped crying and was snuggled up against her mother on the sofa, sucking on a bottle. Scarlett was staring at the mantelpiece, and a photo of herself, the baby, and a man.

'That'll keep the flowers fresh until the funeral.'

'Thanks.'

'Can I smoke in front of the child?'

'I don't care.'

'Cheers.'

I opened the window, lit up, and blew smoke rings into the oblivious air.

'So who's the guy in the photo?'

Scarlett sighed.

'That's Pearse Mahon. Alison's dad. My boyfriend. Well, fiancé. He hasn't always—I mean—look, I'm not going to pretend he didn't hit me. He doesn't make a habit of it. He broke down and cried like a baby afterwards.'

'How many times?'

'I'm not a child.'

'How many more times, Scarlett?'

'Once. Twice.'

The smoke rings dissolved into nothing.

'Twice. After—after Alison. She's almost two now. She needs a daddy.'

'No one needs a daddy. Look, I'm not going to preach. You deserve better, that's all.'

Scarlett laughed.

'What's so funny?'

'Deserve. It's hilarious, all these women talking about what they deserve. They deserve a rich husband, and a house, and never having to work a day in their lives. They deserve getting their hair done every week, getting a manicure and pedicure once a month, and a bunch of tablets to help them shit, sleep and stay thin. They deserve the best schools for their kids, and holidays three times a year, and somebody else to clean their house for them. What makes them so special? Sad fact of life, Jay, some of us take what we can get.'

'You're right. That is sad.'

'You don't get knocked up and walk out because he can't hold his drink. You put up with him because you love him, or at least because you need him, because having a man who hits you is better than having no man at all.'

'Bullshit.'

'Grow up, Jay.'

A car horn blasted outside.

'That'll be your mum,' Scarlett said, standing up with Alison in her arms.

'It's your life, I guess.'

On the spur of the moment, I gave them a hug. Her body shivered against mine, like a bird trapped between the claws of a cat.

'I'm surprised,' I said. 'I thought you'd want something more for Alison.'

I felt like punching glass. Instead, I went out to the car, and buckled myself into the passenger seat. The important thing was always to be somewhere else. We spent half our lives in cars, on planes, on trains, or wishing we were any-where but here, but all the time, we were stuck, stuck with the choices we' d made a long time ago, stuck in the never-ending time-loop of the present, stuck in our own lives.

The irony being, we can't escape ourselves, so we look for distractions anywhere we can, and tell ourselves that the lives we've built – the friends, the social media, the jobs, the online libraries – are who we are. But who would we be if we were stripped of all those things?

Dolores drove with a cigarette in one hand, curling her lip as she looked back at Scarlett's house in the rear-view mirror.

'Is everything OK?'

The image of Scarlett's face returned. Naked. Tender. Sore. The dark bruise stark against the hollowness of her eye. The sharp contour of her cheekbone. The sudden flush of shame when she realised I knew.

'Why didn't you tell me he hits her?'

'What's there to tell? He's just some local lad with quick fists. Good looking, in a slack-jawed sort of way. Works in a garage.'

'Does everyone know about it?'

Dolores cut in front of a car on a blind corner, leaving the other car in the ditch.

'Oh, yes.'

We drove on in silence. The countryside was where it all happened. The wild space, fields and mountains, forests, lakes and bogs, concealed Frank's business premises.

Who would've thought that Frank could plant a spy in one of the largest drinks companies in the world, and get him in a position to relay information back, in microscopic detail, on the recipes they used, the machinery they operated, the finish on the labels of their bottles?

First of all, he'd set up a distillery, including a seven-stage filter for deionising the water used in the distillation process. Then came the bottling, capping and labelling, until the finished product looked no different from the real thing. It almost *was* the real thing. Then he'd undercut prices, selling directly to nightclubs and pubs.

If their customers couldn't tell the difference, who cared? He'd raked in millions from that alone.

Then there was the infamous oil smuggling. With fuel being taxed so much less in the Republic of Ireland, it made sense to buy it there at a cheaper rate, smuggle it across the border, and sell it at a higher price. What Frank did went one step further.

Agricultural diesel cost around one quarter of the price of oil bought at petrol stations. He'd set up a fuel laundering plant, where the agricultural diesel could be chemically treated to wash out the dye put in by the processors, for the very reason that this made it difficult to launder.

Difficult, but not impossible. You could easily double your investment by selling it to petrol stations, where it was sold as ordinary car fuel.

As for the smuggled cigarettes which Dolores scorned, that was even simpler. You bought them by the lorry-load from somewhere with low or zero tax on tobacco products – Thailand, say, or China – shipped them over, and sold them at a mark-up to retailers, while still undercutting the wholesalers. You could get about ten million cigarettes in one forty-foot container, and cream off a profit of one million on each load.

A flock of birds glided overhead.

'Jays,' Dolores said.

Pirating CDs, DVDs, and computer games was a piece of piss. You just needed a burner, a photocopier, and willing middlemen to peddle them.

Dolores turned the radio on. It was tuned to a country music station, the music of choice for bandits, outlaws, and rebels. A man sang about his love for a no-good woman. The twang in his voice and guitar left my heartstrings un-twanged. To me, country music sounds like songs for simpletons – the three chords, the plaintive melodies, the instruments barely put to use, just marking time. And yet lots of people not only love it, but find it moving.

The stories of jealousy, betrayal, misfortune – and, occasionally, real love – ring true to the emotional cores of millions of people. Are they all idiots, running around on primitive impulse? Or am I too cynical to find the simple narratives of folk music of any relevance to my life, rambling, chaotic, and senseless as it is?

I like to think I'm a cut above the common herd, but I know I still belong there. To a lot of the people around me, I'm even lower down the social ladder than they are. I don't have a career, or a wife, or a house, or a family. I tell myself I don't need those things, and despise people who can't talk about anything except their mortgages, their children, their love affairs, their work, but a part of me envies the simplicity of their existence.

The song on the radio changed to something else. It sounded almost exactly the same. Hedges rolled by, and I had the strangest sensation of moving backwards in time.

For a while, there had also been the easier, day-to-day smuggling that had turned a tidy profit. Smuggling sheep and cows over the border from the North to the South allowed farmers to claim a rebate from the Irish republic, the profits from which could be neatly split between farmers and smugglers. That had been an easy gig when border duty – policing the imaginary divide, checking suspicious cars and vehicles, and claiming four times your usual pay for the privilege – had effectively ceased to exist, post-ceasefire.

It was OK for a while, but as agriculture died a death, Frank begun to phase it out.

Meanwhile, Frank diversified, counterfeiting everything from cosmetics to handbags, sports strips to designer socks, aftershave, toothpaste and deodorant, all the while dodging tax and looking for a way to hide the profits.

You couldn't spend it outright, especially since the law allowing the seizing of assets from suspected criminal activity came into being. You couldn't wash it as easily as turning red diesel into white. So what you did was invest it in legitimate businesses, taking care that your name didn't crop up on any documentation.

The easiest way Frank had found to launder huge sums of ready cash was in the property boom of the late Nineties and early Noughties. Offices, restaurants, pubs, clubs, and homes.

Every time you heard about some local lad getting smashed off his face and falling off a fence and breaking his leg or his teeth or dislocating his shoulder, some wag or other was sure to say, 'That's what you get for drinking O'Reilly's vodka, sure it puts you wild.'

Bollocks. If the recipe is the same, then how can there be any harm in it?

A lot of the local lads just can't hold their spirits.

OK, so cleaned diesel won't do your car engine any favours in the long run, but maybe the savings you make in the short term outweigh the cost of a new engine. Maybe you just want to save a few bob every time you need a full tank. So what?

Sometimes you need to worry about how much you're spending today, not how much your decisions will cost you in the future.

My dad's barns processed maybe five million litres of fuel every year, and in all that processing, only a few of the boys had done themselves an injury during the highly dangerous and noxious diesel-cleaning process. If one of them burns out an eye, or blows off a couple of fingers, or carelessly inhales any poisonous fumes, well, the money is worth the risk, and a generous compensation package means everyone is happy.

You take the risk, you hope it pays off, and you pay the price if it doesn't.

The film industry spends hundreds of thousands of dollars on anti-piracy awareness every year, stuffing their official DVD releases full of it, warning cinema goers to report suspicious activity to staff, but the truth is, no one cares if the industry loses a few million.

They can afford to lose money more than you can afford to pay for their product.

I hadn't yet figured out where moving a van fitted into my dad's schemes.

As we approached our driveway, Dolores pressed a switch on her key ring which opened the wrought-iron gates. Home again. We zoomed up the gravel driveway, spraying stones on either side. They fell with a satisfactory pitter-patter and we scrunched to a halt beside Frank's BMW. He climbed out of the car with a broad smile and open arms. Dolores leapt out of her car and into his embrace, standing on tiptoes to peck his cheek, one high heel almost falling from her foot. I appeared beside them.

'I'll take the job,' I said.

Frank put his enormous hand on my shoulder.

'Good decision,' he said, then slapped me on the back.

'OK, boys,' Dolores said. 'Let's have a quick cup of tea before the funeral. Jay, you'd better look over your reading before we get to church.'

On the way inside, Frank stopped to examine a shrub not quite as splendid as those surrounding it. He grabbed it at its base, wrenching it up by the roots with his bare hands. He tossed it over his shoulder onto the gravel.

'One of the lads will sort that out in the morning.'

I stood at the kitchen door, staring down at the black cat I'd seen in the garden earlier that morning. The cat stared back at me with a perfectly feline inscrutability, and dropped a small, brown, very dead bird at my feet.

6

Murder

I arrived early at Aunty Kate's house, scanning the crowd for Scarlett's blonde head. I smiled politely and shook hands with the obscure relatives who were there for breakfast. I slowly pressed my way through to the kitchen. Scarlett wasn't there, but another cousin was, doling out bacon and eggs to rheumy-eyed uncles and tired children. She silently handed me a bacon sandwich with brown sauce. It had always been my favourite. I thanked her, although I couldn't remember her name, and went to wait in the living room.

Friends, neighbours and relatives arrived in dribs and drabs. Television, music and radio were forbidden luxuries you had to do without during wakes, and the house had an unnatural quietness, especially now, without booze. I had spent the entire night thinking about Duncan's death. The very words had played at the back of my mind like an old man playing the bodhrán.

Dead. Dead. Dead. Dead. Duncan's dead. Duncan's dead.

I tried to concentrate on the living.

Seamus prayed with his head bent at a holy candle on the mantelpiece, candlelight glittering in his hair. He crossed himself and blew out the candle. I followed him to the wake room. We were truly alone, with only Duncan's coffin, an overhead light, and empty chairs backed against the walls for company. It was difficult to fathom the absolute silence. It was almost as if the silence had been there all along, waiting in a cloud above our heads, ready to slowly descend upon us like snow, once its chance had come.

Seamus and I stood perfectly still, staring at the coffin as if something was going to happen. The electric light hummed gently. The coffin remained solid and closed. You heard stories about dead men sitting up in their coffins, or farting loudly during the ceremonies, all part of the natural phenomena that happened after death. I was half expecting it. It was the sort of embarrassing thing Duncan would do. It might help ease the tension.

But no, the coffin was silent and unmoving.

I contemplated the coffin. Handsome wood. Ornate fittings. A reassuring solidity, for those scared by the idea of their loved ones becoming worm food. Why did it matter to people to preserve the memories of their dead, and their bodies?

Was it the thought of the slow decomposition, the bit-by-bit disappearance of tissues and flesh, which upset stable minds, and urged them to splash out on coffins offering protection against the elements of nature they found distressing?

Maybe the rationale went that at least they could rest easy knowing that dear Aunty Margaret looked lovely in her silk-lined mahogany number, a little pale perhaps, but stunning nonetheless?

All that nasty falling-apart business could be safely delayed until – inevitably – it was the turn of those she'd left behind to rot.

These things did matter when you were alive though. No

matter how rational you wanted to be, no matter how dispassionate and modern and free of superstition, you still wanted a good life for you and those you loved.

One hundred grand would go a long way, if I was careful with it.

I could buy a car. I could take a holiday, somewhere I'd never been. I could put a deposit on a flat. It was enough money to start over with, change my life, give me a little security for a few years, while I worked on getting a better job, or moving somewhere nicer, or considered settling down. But that was selfish. I knew someone who needed the money more than me.

How much would it take for Scarlett to escape from Pearse, get out of her council house, and take her daughter with her? If we split the money fifty-fifty, it would still be enough for us both to start over with. We could even disappear together if we wanted to, London or somewhere, set up house, raise the baby, find jobs we didn't mind. Yeah.

I could make that happen, for both of us. It might even help ease the gnawing feeling that my dad was keeping something from me.

'The priest's here.'

'I need a cigarette.'

'Tuck your shirt in, Jay.'

'Cigarette first,' I said.

Seamus shrugged and left the room. I could hear the unlovely music of Aunty Kate's vocal pipes interspersed with the lilting flute of Fr Flaherty's less strident instrument. I scratched my balls, sniffed my armpits and went outside for a smoke.

It was an ordinary sort of day, and an ordinary sort of

day was good enough for Duncan. I lit up. Smoke rushed through my lungs, warm and welcome, like the first flush of love across the face of a beautiful girl. As I flicked ash into the yard and gratefully sucked on death's nicotine kiss, a youth drove up in a badly dented car. It took me a couple of seconds to register that Scarlett was in the passenger seat, and Alison was shaking her rattle in the back. I tossed my cigarette aside. They parked.

I took the measure of Pearse Mahon.

Shifty eyes, shaved head, his mouth a straight line in a hard face. He might age well, if I didn't break his face first. Scarlett was skilfully made up. No bruise was visible around her eye. She introduced us nervously.

'Jay, Pearse, Pearse, Jay.'

'Sorry for your trouble,' Pearse said, offering his hand.

I hesitated, and then shook hands, crushing Pearse's fingers just a little too hard.

He didn't flinch.

They went inside. I stayed outside to shake more hands at the door as neighbours arrived to accompany the body to church. As the undertakers prepared the coffin for the hearse, the rhythmic murmur of prayers rose through the house, led by Fr Flaherty. The words were known to us all by heart, their pattern familiar, yet the prayers themselves had probably ceased to have any meaning beyond the comfortable ritual of their repetition. Some of us looked at our phones, tapped our feet, or whispered amongst ourselves.

I helped carry the coffin to the hearse. Six of us, brothers and cousins, hefted Duncan onto our shoulders, as the undertaker deftly flitted in and around us. I was left and middle, and surprised at how light the coffin was.

The hearse crawled along the street, the family following directly behind, friends and neighbours next, as bystanders and passers-by watched. I was with Dolores and Frank near the head of the procession. Dolores slipped her arm through mine. I didn't mind.

People stopped going about their business to watch and cross themselves. Cars slowed down as we passed. At the church, we hoisted the coffin up on our shoulders once more and climbed the steep steps to the top of the hill. A helicopter trailing a box of supplies in a net for the army barracks whirred lazily overhead.

Fr Flaherty took his place at the altar. Four boys flanked him in their red-and-white robes, trying to look pious. We put the coffin on a brass stand in front of the altar. Then we took our seats, and the priest said all the usual things that priests say at funerals.

'Death is a shock to us all . . . Our normal lives are apprehended, as we wonder what has become of our loved one . . . Faith in God sustains us at times like these . . .'

Candles. Incense. Light filtered through stained glass windows, casting harlequin patterns on the floor. I was mildly surprised to see that there was still a men's gallery and a women's gallery, where the gender divide was strictly adhered to, even down to toddlers going with their same-sex parent to watch the ceremony from above.

'Duncan Goodman was not a special man. He was not a celebrity. He had never been on television, or played in a band, or written a book . . .'

I wondered if Martin was in the church, as bored as I was.

'. . . but he was one of us, a family man, a local man, a

simple man amongst simple people. And we are happy to be simple people, safe in God's love, and we trust he has a plan for each and every one of us . . .'

Over my shoulder, Alison began to wail.

'. . . and now, the prayers of the faithful.'

I remembered to genuflect, and read the prayer without embarrassing myself.

I saw Duncan's ex-wife and their children sitting slightly back from the rest of the family. His children were crying. His ex-wife was not. I nodded at her. She blanked me. Scarlett also avoided my eyes as I slid back to my seat. I stayed in my seat during Communion.

At the end of the indoors part, I shouldered my burden for the final time, and we carried the coffin to a brand-new plot in the cemetery.

The burial is always the most miserable part of the service. You have to stand around outside whatever the weather, listen to more inane words, shake dozens more hands than you'd already shaken, and watch the coffin being lowered into the ground only for it to be covered up with fake plastic grass, until you dispersed, leaving the groundsmen to fill in the earth while you were all having tea.

The reception was being held in the football club. A buffet was laid out at the back of the room, two local girls on hand to serve tea and coffee, as the caterer shared her condolences and her food. The ubiquitous plates of sandwiches and cake were supplemented with sausage rolls and chicken skewers. Big-bellied men unbuttoned their suit jackets. Expensively groomed women shook their bangles and chemically enhanced hair. The smugglers and their expensive, interchangeable girlfriends looked happy. I was hungry, filled my plate, and sat down with Seamus, Scarlett, Pearse and Alison.

'The weather held up, anyway,' Pearse said.

'They've put on a decent spread,' Seamus said.

'It'll only hit Aunty Kate now that the burial's over,' Scarlett said.

'Wah wah,' Alison said, with no more or less originality than her elders.

They opened the bar – pints for the men, wine or vodka for the ladies.

As the funeral was over, we were allowed to watch TV. One of the barmen flicked on a news channel on the large flat-screen telly that dominated the front of the hall. Chatter erupted and people began to mingle. Heads turned as a small, skinny man, bent almost double in haste, ran into the room, making a beeline for Frank.

'Who's that?'

'Shush.'

Frank leaned over to let the gatecrasher hiss in his ear. At the same time, the TV news presenter cleared his throat, and spoke into the sudden hush that had fallen over the hall.

'News has just come in about a fatal shooting in Newry, County Down. As yet, the dead man has not been formally identified. Police have no suspects at this time. It is not known if there is any paramilitary involvement. More news on that breaking story as it comes.'

From across the room, I watched in horror as the whole world shrank to the broad grin spreading across Frank's face. I half rose from my chair. Scarlett put her hand on my arm, and I fell back down again.

Frank turned towards us, looked me straight in the eye, and winked.

The facts emerged in bits and pieces, like all gossip. The first version of the story bore the bare bones of truth dressed up in speculation, further pieces being added later as more news leaked from those in the know and those watching on the margins. It took some hours for an approximate picture of what really happened to become the accepted reality.

What really happened was that at 10 AM on the morning of Duncan Goodman's funeral, Lisa Murphy, girlfriend of Ian 'Muck' McGinley, was kidnapped as she was leaving her home to keep a hairdresser's appointment. Two men, dressed casually in leather jackets and jeans, grabbed her by the arms and bundled her into the back of a waiting van, driven by a third man. There were no windows in the back of the van.

She was forced to kneel, facing the back doors of the vehicle, as the men blindfolded her, bound her wrists and ankles, and punched her repeatedly to shut her up. Bewildered, bleeding, convinced she was going to die, Lisa lay sobbing on the gritty floor of the van, with no idea of where they were driving to or, apparently, who these men were, or why they had targeted her.

The men cracked jokes about raping her in turn before putting a bullet in the back of her head. She heard their guns cock.

Afterwards, Lisa said she could not recall how long they had driven for. It could have been five minutes. It could have been an hour. Prayers spooled on a loop through her mind, *'Please don't let them kill me, Jesus, please don't let them rape me, God, please don't let them kill me.'*

She publicly credited divine intervention for sparing her life. The truth was, killing Lisa Murphy had never been the kidnappers' intention.

They stopped. Lisa was bundled out and thrown on the ground.

Did they say anything?

'Any last words?'

'There's three of us, darling, we could all fuck a different hole at once.'

'Get the phone.'

Did they say anything else?

Yes, lots of other stuff, but she couldn't remember what.

Were they physically violent?

They kicked her, dragged her in the mud. She remembered thinking her hair would look awful when they discovered her body because she'd never made it to the hairdresser's. Her mouth tasted of blood and fear.

One of the men dialled a number on a mobile phone – it wasn't pre-entered, she heard the beeps as the numbers were pressed – and the phone was held to her face as she lay there, bound in the dirt.

'Tell him exactly what we say.'

'What we tell you, bitch.'

The phone rang.

'H-hello?'

'Ian? Oh God, Ian—'

'You're at the crossroads where he keeps his stash. You're at his stash house.'

'I'm at your stash house, at the crossroads . . .'

'We're going to kill you if he doesn't get here in the next twenty minutes. Alone.'

'Ian, Jesus, Ian, they're going to shoot me, Ian!'

'Tell him to get here in the next twenty minutes.'

'They say you've got to get here in the next twenty minutes—'

'Alone.'

'Alone!'

'Or else.'

'They've got guns, they'll do it, they'll kill me—'

The phone went dead.

Twenty minutes of near silence. No traffic. Lisa tried to think of where they were, but gave up. Would he come? Would they kill her anyway? Would they kill them both? Money, it had to be money – but why didn't they ask for money on the phone?

The men did not speak, but she heard them take things out of the van, as if they were preparing the ground for something.

Lisa heard her boyfriend's car arrive.

Ian McGinley had come to his stash house at the crossroads.

He had come alone.

He was not armed.

In all likelihood, he was probably expecting a negotiation for money. He may have expected some form of intimidation. He may or may not have responded to threats. He never got the chance.

She heard him say, 'Lads?' nervously.

Did he mention any names?

No, no, no.

Did he sound as if he recognised them?

No, how could she tell, no. They were strangers, how could he have recognised them?

When Ian McGinley's body was discovered, it turned out that he'd been tortured before he was shot.

Knees shattered. Left shoulder dislocated. Right arm broken. Jaw dislocated. Skull fractured. Blood, piss, shit, vomit, everywhere. A bullet to the back of the head, which had taken half his face off on exit.

It was likely that Lisa Murphy, bound nearby, had heard the three men torture and kill her lover. She couldn't remember. All the doctors said she was suffering from post-traumatic stress.

She remembered the van leaving.

She lay there, she didn't know how long.

She came to. She freed herself. She discovered her lover's body. She knelt in his brains and cradled his broken corpse in her lap and wept. She found her handbag, her phone, and called her mother.

'And she knows rightly who it was, too.'

'Sure how do we know she wasn't up to her neck in it?'

'No better than she ought to be, either. It's the wife I feel sorry for, with that whore all over the news and her husband not even cold.'

News of the murder filtered through the TV, the radio, my neighbours' lips. Even as we sat in the football club as the story first broke, phones erupted with news of the killing, and guests not connected to the smuggling trade seemed to remember important social obligations elsewhere, leaving early enough to avoid being present should the police arrive to question Frank O'Reilly and his cronies.

In a daze, I went to the shop to buy smokes. On my way,

I passed whispering women and wide-eyed men, who stopped to swap the latest morsels of gossip. They all had something to say to us about McGinley. In private, they all knew Frank was guilty of murder. I kept going over last night in the pub, how Dolores had said not to worry about it, how Frank had everything under control. I smoked outside the football club, and time passed as if it was happening to someone else.

I walked Scarlett to her car, in case photographers or journalists were lurking nearby. Scarlett looked scared as she kissed me goodbye, pale beneath her makeup. Pearse looked sick, his shifty eyes looking up and down the road and over his shoulder before he got into the car. Alison waved her rattle and gurgled.

'I'm scared, Jay.'

'I'll think of something. I promise.'

I somehow managed to say all the right things as the funeral party broke up.

'Such a way to go,' a woman said on the way out the door. 'Tortured! It doesn't bear thinking about.'

'Best not to talk about it,' her husband said.

'We all know what sort of a man he was, but still, you wouldn't wish that on your worst enemy, would you?'

'Best be going,' the husband said, putting an arm around his good lady wife and marching her out of the hall.

He cast one final glance over his shoulder as he went.

I smiled in what I hoped was a pleasant, non-murderous fashion.

The man fell over a chair in his haste to exit the building.

Driving home, the radio kept us up to date with the latest developments.

Frank chuckled from time to time. Dolores looked out the passenger window, her hand resting lightly on Frank's knee, a half smile playing on her lips, her eyes preoccupied.

I kept my mouth shut.

Back home, Dolores kissed Frank on the cheek and went straight inside.

'Wait,' Frank said, as I opened the door.

'Why?'

'My car and my jeep are the only two places that definitely aren't bugged.'

Frank cracked his knuckles. I saw a flash of McGinley's kneecap shatter.

'You want to know why I'm paying you one hundred grand to get rid of a van. Simple. It's the murder van.'

I'd known that since the news broke.

'There's nothing to worry about. We've got alibis. We were at the funeral. There are literally hundreds of witnesses who can put us there, in plain sight, while that stupid fucker got what was coming to him.'

Sweat dripped down Frank's forehead. He wiped it off with his sleeve.

'Any questions?'

When did you go completely mad? was what I didn't say.

'Why not just burn the van?'

Frank chortled.

'Good man! Because they can pick up all sorts of evidence from burnt-out vans these days. Forensics, you know? Burning it isn't enough. It has to disappear.'

Frank snapped his fingers. I saw a flash of McGinley's arm snapping in two.

'Besides, do you think they'd be above planting evidence?

Not on your life. No, better to make the van disappear altogether. They're not getting this fly bastard, and that's a fact.'

Frank's eyes scanned my face from the rear-view mirror.

'Son, I know you must be feeling a bit fucked-up right now. So you didn't see this coming. So what? It's not on your head. It's your old man's doing. You're doing this as a favour for me. You know what?'

'Tell me.'

'I was going to get Muck to bring a ransom with him. I was thinking, yeah, the fucker can bring one hundred grand of his own cash, and that'll cover the cost of Jay losing the van. But you know what?'

'What?'

'I said to myself, nah, Jay wouldn't go for that. Wouldn't take blood money out of a dead man's hand. Look at it this way. The money you're going to earn, straight out of my pocket, will make up for all the years you turned your back on this family. Agreed?'

As if I had a choice.

'Agreed.'

'Good. I knew I could rely on you, son.'

Then Frank hefted his bulk out of the car, slamming the door with an almighty whack.

I saw a flash of McGinley's skull cracking, and had no idea what to do.

7

Egg and Chips

'There you go love, egg and chips. Mind your fingers, it's hot.' I stared down at my plate. Chips as big as fingers. White slime all across them.

I picked up the ketchup and dashed off a couple of red zigzags across the gelatinous splatter of my lunch. Martin grimaced.

'Egg and ketchup on one plate. Yuk.'

'It's art,' I said.

'It's a bloody mess.'

'Come on. What does that look like to you?'

'How can you eat that? The colours clash. Gross.'

'I'm asking you,' I said, pointing to my plate, 'what does that look like to you?'

Martin shrugged.

'Egg and chips.'

'Look again.'

'I dunno. Egg and chips.'

'It's a fucking masterpiece, is what it is.'

'You mean like Jackson Pollock?'

'It's art. What it represents is several guys all having a wank and then they've got their hands chopped off. Maybe they're Muslims, they do that there, don't they? Look. Fingers, cum and blood everywhere. The critics will lap it up, fake bodily fluids and everything. I should enter that for the Turner Prize.'

Martin shook his head.

'You're setting off my food-Asperger's. I feel sick.'

I poked my knife into the yolk of the egg. Yellow oozed into the mix.

'One of the blokes had gonorrhoea,' I said.

'Nah. Gonorrhoea's green. I think.'

I stared through the window on which flaking paint read 'Sylvia's Diner' backwards, superimposed across the scene outside like an extra layer of film in an old cartoon. A toothless man led a pit bull terrier on a leash, blurred tattoos bleeding into sagging skin. A woman sucked the last dying gasp from a cigarette, flicked it into the gutter, and trotted out of sight on leopard-print high heels the same colours as her bleached-blonde hair and dark roots.

A tracksuited couple ambled by with a baby in a pushchair. He looked into the diner – no, he was checking his reflection in the window. The baby bounced and its mother picked a soft toy from a selection on its lap and waggled it in its face. Light caught the matching ear studs of all three members of the family, casting golden splinters into the air, where they pinwheeled, and were gone.

'Ever want,' I said, my eyes still outdoors, 'to disappear?'

'You what?'

'Disappear. Get away. Vamoose.'

'From what?'

'This. Life.'

Martin had just bitten into his bacon sandwich. He stopped chewing, his mouth hanging open.

'Brown sauce,' I said. 'Why don't you have any brown sauce on that sandwich? Everyone likes brown sauce on bacon sandwiches.'

Martin put his sandwich down carefully on his plate, chewed, and swallowed. He wiped his mouth with a napkin and sipped his tea.

'I hate ketchup. I hate mayonnaise. I really fucking hate brown sauce. What is brown sauce anyway? What flavour is it supposed to be?'

The waitress dropped an extra napkin at Martin's elbow.

'Brown flavour,' I said. 'What flavour do you think?'

'But what is it?'

I shrugged.

'Tell him none of your sauce, love,' the waitress said with a wink at Martin.

Martin laughed. I sighed. The waitress rolled her eyes and went to another table.

We were sitting in Sylvia's Diner because I'd rolled up to Martin's doorstep that afternoon. I hadn't slept in twenty-four hours, my hair was a mess, my clothes were crumpled, and I smelled a bit ripe around the armpits. Martin had taken me into town rather than invite me in, because he knew very well what was wrong. He'd heard about the murder.

Who hadn't?

Town was the same as always. Despite murder on your doorstep, life went on. You still had to eat, drink, and work. Curious eyes followed us as we walked down the street together, Martin trying to keep the conversation neutral until we could talk somewhere relatively quiet. The diner was a dingy little spot, a favourite of the afternoon sausage, beans-and-chips brigade, who were not to be swayed by the fancy delights of the Chinese restaurant, curry, or aspirational pre-packed sandwiches.

'My mum won't eat anything that isn't based on potato,' Martin had confided as we crossed the threshold. 'It's as if the famine never happened.'

I was staring into space.

'Look, never mind brown sauce. What's eating you?'

I pushed my plate away.

'I want to get away. I'm sick of everything. I want to get away from other people's mortgages and stepping over needles in the street. I want out of waiting for a better job to come along, waiting for the right girl, wondering if I'll ever settle down. I want to live in a country where the government aren't in it for the money and the voting public don't vote with their wallets, or coz they're scared of backing the losing team, and actually give a shit when they find out their elected representatives are on the take. I want to get away from girls in fairy wings puking in the streets and lads pissing up against walls in broad daylight. I want to live in a country that speaks its own language and doesn't apologise for it. I want to live wherever knives aren't shoved down bootstraps and shit celebrities don't live on TV and we don't kiss the Pope's arse for covering up kiddie-fiddling clerics for years on end. I want an escape hatch. I want to be invisible. I want the chance to start again.'

I slumped back into my chair.

'I don't think that's the real problem,' Martin said. 'Take it from the top.'

I took a deep breath.

'OK. You heard about You Know What?'

'Keep your voice down.'

'They're all listening anyway.'

'Jay, either shut up, or keep your voice down. No one's listening if you don't let them.'

Several pairs of eyes swivelled away from our table as Martin glared around the room.

'Right. Well. You know about You Know What?'

Martin nodded.

'Well, it turns out that the other thing I said I'd do for my dad is connected to it.'

Martin nodded again.

I was suddenly grateful for the noise of the radio in the background broadcasting the chattering inanities of listeners on a phone-in competition, the clatter of knives and forks on plates that squealed when scraped, the traffic rolling by.

I continued.

'So I've promised the old man I'll do it. I can't get out of it now. But it puts me in the frame if anything goes wrong. If I'm caught, I'm connected to You Know What. And if I don't do it . . .'

'Can't you just tell your dad you won't do it?'

I shook my head.

'It's not that simple.'

'There'd be nothing he could do about it. You could stay out of it, as he's changed the nature of the game.'

A man came in, shaking and wheezing. He took his cap off, stamped his feet on the thin mat at the door, and looked around with a smile on his broken face. White whiskers stood out stark against his ruddy complexion. Several patrons nodded at him.

'Hello, Francie, the usual is it?'

'Yes, aye, yes, the usual it is.'

'How are you today, Francie?'

'Aye, thanks, not so bad, yeah. Ha ha.'

'Now, here you go, Francie, chips with salt and vinegar, just the way you like them, love.'

Francie shuffled over to the counter, the smile never straying from his lips, not even so far as his eyes, which rolled from side to side as if in constant battle with each other. He stank of piss and booze.

'No money today—' he began, but the waitress cut him off.

'Get me again tomorrow Francie, alright?'

'Broke, sorry—'

'You can pay for them tomorrow, love, alright?'

'Thanks, thanks.'

'No bother, love. Take care. Bye-bye Francie.'

'Bye-bye.'

'Tis a pity of him all the same,' a woman said, as the door swung closed behind Francie's back. Then he loped off, and no one thought about him again.

I stared glumly at my plate.

Martin munched on his sandwich and sipped his tea.

'The thing is,' I said, 'I really want the money.'

'Right.'

'It's not all for me,' I said. 'Some of it's for Scarlett. But the thing is, the money's just sitting there. Someone's going to get it, and You Know What has already happened. Nothing can change that, right? So why shouldn't I just do this one thing, take the money, and run?'

'Escape.'

'Right.'

'Go for it,' Martin said with a shrug.

'What?'

'Go for it. Why shouldn't you?'

'Coz . . . Fuck it, I know it's wrong!'

'Keep your voice down, Jay.'

'Sorry. I know it's wrong,' I said, quietly.

'So what? Look. The money's going begging, you agreed to do this thing before you knew the terms and conditions, you want the cash. It's not your fault your dad is who he is. If you say you don't have a choice in the matter, I believe you. So do it. Make the best of a bad situation. Take the money and fuck off, escape, or help Scarlett, or do whatever it is you want to do.'

'Do you really think that?'

'I really do.'

'Oh.'

'Now eat your bloody chips, they're getting cold-looking. I hate congealed food. It's putting me off my sandwich.'

'I don't like egg and chips.'

'What are you talking about?'

'Egg and chips. Can't stand them.'

'Why the hell did you order them, then?'

'Coz, we're here. You know. Greasy spoon. It seemed like the thing to do.'

'You ordered them because you thought you ought to?'

'It's what you eat in a place like this.'

'You don't have to eat egg and chips because you saw it on *Corrie*.'

'I thought I might like it, once I had it in front of me.'

'You could've ordered, I don't know, soup or something. Something nice and bland.'

'I mean, what are eggs anyway, when you think about them?'

'Oh hang on, it's tomato soup today. I can't stand tomato soup, it looks like a bowl of blood.'

'They're just hens' periods, aren't they? Little dead potential chickens. Can you imagine eating the menstrual cycle of any other animal?'

'Jay, seriously, I'm trying to eat.'

'Sorry, but come on. Egg and fucking chips.'

'You ordered it.'

'Don't even start me on the chips. Bloody potatoes, man. First we all ate them, then the crops failed, then we fucking starved coz the Brits wouldn't let us eat anything else . . .'

'Huh?'

'. . . and then, like, what? Two-thirds of the population died out or emigrated? And now we still want to stuff our faces with potatoes.'

'Well, that's what I was saying when we got here. It's like the famine never happened.'

'Exactly! You'd think we'd fucking ban spuds or something, instead of making them the basis of every national dish.'

'You just can't persuade the good people of Ireland to look beyond what they're used to. They'll eat cockles and mussels, but try selling them sushi.'

'It's all take what you're given, and like it.'

'It's all downtrodden Catholic gratitude.'

'Big time. Big time.'

I harpooned a chip, and then another, stuffing them in my face without thinking. I cut a splattery bit off my egg with the blunt edge of my fork and rammed it in my mouth.

I sploshed some tea and milk into my mug, dashed in some sugar from the dispenser, and slurped down a mouthful, satisfied.

'So, what you said about the Irish language?'

'What did I say about it?'

'How you want to live in a country where you speak your own language and don't have to apologise for it.'

'Well, yeah.'

'What did you mean?'

'I don't know.'

'Don't be ridiculous. You said it. You must know what you meant.'

I chewed some egg and chip thoughtfully before replying.

'Doesn't it bother you even a little that we all speak English, and no one except for a few poor bastards in Donegal remember how to converse in what's supposed to be our native tongue?'

'That's not true.'

'Isn't it?'

'Irish is still compulsory at school down South. Everyone there speaks a little.'

'But isn't it depressing, how quickly a culture can be wiped out?'

'British culture's been dying on its arse for decades, even if we do speak English.'

'That,' I said, shovelling more food in my gob, 'is small comfort.'

'Besides, I like that Irish hasn't gone global. You can talk about people in public when you're on holidays, and no one has a clue what you're on about.'

'Wow. You must be a riot on holidays.'

'Oh, shut up. Guess who I met here one day?'

'Who?'

'My dad.'

'Oh?'

'Yeah. I landed a big job, took my mum here for a big, fuck-off fry-up to celebrate. Next thing you know, this big swarthy gypsy with salt-and-pepper hair comes striding in. Flynn Furey. Mum near died.'

'What happened?'

'He didn't see us, at first. He sweeps up to the girl at the counter and says, "Hello darling, you're looking lovely." "Oh don't look at me," she says, "I look like a gypsy." '

'Ouch.'

'She was mortified. "Oh I didn't mean any offence," she says, "we have gypsies in here all the time." He just laughed.'

'So what happened next?'

'That was the weird part. Next thing you know, I heard myself speaking, without even realising I'd opened my mouth. I said, "Yeah, I'm half gypsy, and I'm here all the time." My dad turned around. He did a double take. Looked at me, my hair, my clothes. He didn't look once at my mum.'

'And?'

'And he said, "Martin." "Hello Dad," I said. "Well," he said. "You know what," he said. "You can't be half gypsy and half a man as well." "What's that supposed to mean," I said. He said, "You know what I mean. I've heard what you get up to. No son of mine goes with other men. You're no son of mine, and you're no gypsy either." '

'Frig. What did you say to that?'

'I said, "I'd rather be a faggot than turn my back on my family." He turned bright red, right to the roots of his hair, and stalked out. "Yeah," I shouted after him: "Walk away. Again." '

'You should put that in a book, I'm telling you.'

'Maybe I will, some day.'

'Go for it. You'll make yourself out to be some big hero, won't you?'

'Yeah, I sure will. I'm great, that's why. I can put in the bit about the time the cops gay-bashed me, and I broke one fucker's nose.'

'Yeah?'

Martin polished off the last bite of his sandwich and leaned across the table.

'Long story. You'd better hope the cops are more civil with you.'

'What do you mean?'

'They're going to be all over your family in the next day or two. I bet your mum and Dad can keep their mouths shut, but it's time you learned how.'

'I can keep my mouth shut,' I said, and finished off my egg and chips in silence.

8

Cops

I was in my bedroom, lying on my bed with my hands behind my head, staring at the ceiling. I was trying hard to think about nothing. It wasn't working. Images of Muck McGinley's dead body kept flashing across my mind. Every time I switched on the TV or checked my phone, more news about the murder leaked into my life. It was impossible to forget it, despite Martin's good advice about keeping my mouth shut. That was the easy part. The hard part was knowing what not to say when the cops came round to interrogate my family.

We knew the cops were on their way.

I'd never liked the cops much. It wasn't so much a reaction to a personally harrowing experience as an instinctive distrust of authority figures with weapons.

'I don't hate anyone in this town,' Frank used to say, 'except those fuckers up in the barracks, and the cops you see walking around town as if they own the place. I don't care if you're black, yellow or purple, as long as you're not a Brit.'

The tolerance Frank claimed to extend to purple people didn't extend to gays, women, or Travellers. In Frank's mind, they weren't real people at all. He didn't greet women in public, or shake hands with tinkers at fairs, or look the local gay couples in the eye.

Frank moved through a world where people like him were in charge.

I wondered if there was much difference between the sort of person Frank was, and the sort of people who became cops.

If one was rigid, authoritarian and violent, so were the others. Two sides of the same coin, on one side the Queen's head, on the other, the harp.

Everyone was scrabbling for coins.

'James!'

I swung my legs over the edge of the bed, sprang up, and snapped to attention.

I only had to hold my nerve. Be calm. Keep my mouth shut.

I crossed the landing to my parents' bedroom.

Everything in it was white, from the white cotton sheets and white cotton pillows, to the white wooden headboard, with white plastic rosary beads hanging from my mum's side of the bed. White wool carpet, white painted walls without art of any kind, white papered ceiling centred with a white linen lampshade.

The white linen curtains were drawn.

I crossed the room and looked out the window, in time to see the cop cars crunch through the gates, spraying gravel as they tore hungry strips through the driveway.

'We need you downstairs, darling!'

I took a deep breath.

Casting a final glance around the room, as if it could help, I automatically straightened the black-and-white photo that sat in a glass frame on the glass-topped table on my dad's side of the bed, a picture of Frank, Dolores and myself on my sixteenth birthday.

Our younger selves beamed at me.

'Coming.'

Dolores was in the hallway, dressed down in designer jeans and a jumper. She opened the door just as a shadow behind the glass was about to knock. There were three of them. The police officers were taken by surprise. The one in charge looked from Dolores to me.

I joined my mum in the doorway. She smiled at the policemen.

'Hello, officers, do come in – once you've shown us your identification.'

The one in charge tensed his jaw, managed a tight smile, and drew his ID from his pocket. The two men behind him, both younger and shorter than their boss, did likewise.

A brace of police officers were still in their cars, parked in our driveway, eyes trained on the house. I wondered if they were fingering their holsters, or if that only happened in films.

'Chief Superintendent James Monaghan. I'm investigating the abduction of Lisa Murphy and the murder of Ian McGinley. You may have heard about these incidents.'

'Absolutely shocking. Of course, we'll help you in any way we can, although I don't think you'll find much of interest from us. Sorry, where are my manners? I'm Dolores O'Reilly – but I expect you knew that, didn't you? – and this is my son, James. He recently came home from Dublin for his cousin's funeral. I'm afraid we're all still very upset about our own family tragedy.'

'My condolences,' Monaghan said, without a hint of sincerity. 'Is Frank O'Reilly at home? we 'd like to speak to all three of you together.'

'Follow me.'

Dolores led the way to the rarely used drawing room, where Frank sat on the sofa. His arms were folded across his belly, a smile on his face. The room was decked out in an unwelcoming shade of turquoise. The furniture was too new to be called comfortable. The watercolours of local beauty spots were technically accomplished, but lacking passion or flair. It was a room for formal occasions, or guests whom Dolores hoped would not stay long.

Dolores sat beside Frank. I stood against the marble fireplace, which had not felt a fire inside it for a very long time. Monaghan stood at the door, flanked by his junior officers. The youngest one made a deliberate display of producing a notebook and pen, flicking through the pages, and poising the nib carefully above a blank sheet.

Dolores watched the pantomime with the sympathetic smile I remembered from her watching children sing badly in my school plays. Frank sat completely still. I quelled the urge to light a cigarette.

'Where were you all two mornings ago, on the day that Lisa Murphy was abducted, and Ian McGinley killed?'

'At my nephew's funeral, as you well know,' Frank said. 'And a big funeral it was too. My nephew Seamus had stayed in the wake house with his cousin and his aunt the night before. We were at home. Me and Dolores and Jay had breakfast here first, before the funeral, then went to the wake house – what time was it?'

'About eight o' clock, dear.'

'Yeah, and Fr Flaherty was there already, along with a couple of dozen mourners who were gathering to say prayers for the soul of my nephew, may he rest in peace.'

'We are confident your alibis for the time in question are sound,' Monaghan said, 'but we haven't yet ruled out the possibility that the men who carried out the kidnapping and murder were under contract by a third party.'

Stay calm. You knew that was coming. They can't prove a thing.

'Do you know a man by the name of John McDonald?'

Dolores and Frank pretended to think.

'John McDonald?' Dolores said.

'Would he be one of the Canary McDonalds?'

'A friend of the Flahertys, you mean?'

'Aye, and probably a friend of Fr Flaherty, wouldn't he be?'

'Unless you're mixing them up with the Lofty McDonalds. Now they were a different shower altogether.'

'John McDonald,' Monaghan said, 'of Saint Michael's Estate, Newry.'

'Never heard of him,' Frank said.

'We keep ourselves to ourselves.'

'Wouldn't have much truck with those Newry boys.'

'Can't trust them, can you? Well, I mean, Mr Monaghan must suspect this John McDonald was up to his neck in this business.'

'Tut-tut.'

'And you, Mr O'Reilly?' Monaghan said, turning to me.

'No.'

'You've never heard of John McDonald?'

'No. Doesn't ring any bells. Sorry.'

'I see. If I were to put it to you all that John McDonald was a member of a gang with known associations to criminals in South Armagh – some of whom have been linked to your name – would that jog your memories?'

Frank's expression did not change.

Dolores smiled pityingly at the policeman.

I felt my hands tremble in my pockets.

'You must be clutching at very thin straws if you think you can come around here and intimidate us,' Frank said, 'with your known associations and your links. What do you take me for? Do you think I was born yesterday?'

'We don't know who you're talking about,' Dolores said, putting a hand on Frank's knee, 'but we understand you're just doing your job. Our names have come up, however erroneously, or by malicious intent by some jealous person in town. Well, by all means, you must ask us questions. It's just too droll. Please, go on.'

'We have reason to believe that Ian McGinley was involved in the smuggling of contraband across the border. It has come to our attention that his sons have been involved in several brawls with employees of yours, Mr O'Reilly, who are employed on your various farms and in some businesses. Could you share any insights you may have into the relationship between your men and the McGinley family?'

Frank remained unmoved. 'I know nothing about it.'

'You haven't heard anything about the animosity between your employees and the McGinleys?'

'No.'

'You remain in a state of ignorance about the McGinleys' constant goading, fighting and provocation of your work-force?'

'Why shouldn't I?'

'You admit to no knowledge of the fact that a feud has been brewing between factions of men whom we have strong reason to believe are key players in the smuggling strongholds of South Armagh?'

'You seem to know more about it than I do.'

'I find that hard to believe.'

'It's not your job to believe. It's your job to gather evidence.'

'I will, Mr O'Reilly. This has gone beyond a tax dodge, gone beyond fraud, gone beyond hiding dirty money in clean investments. This is murder, and conspiracy to murder.'

Frank was silent. Dolores was no longer smiling, but her fingers gripped Frank's, bleaching his knuckles white. I knew my own face was panicked.

'Mr O'Reilly,' Monaghan said, turning to me again. 'I believe you witnessed an altercation between the McGinley brothers and other locals, some of whom are employed by your father, in a pub in Crossmaglen two days before the murder?'

I wetted my lips. I looked to my parents. They looked back impassively.

'It's a simple question, Mr O'Reilly. Did you or did you not witness an altercation between the McGinley brothers, sons of the murdered Ian McGinley, and various local men who work for your father in certain capacities?'

I cleared my throat.

'I did see the McGinley brothers in town. They were drunk and rowdy. I had no idea who they were, until they picked a fight with some people at the table beside them. I think someone knocked over a drink, and that's how it started, but I wasn't really paying attention. I couldn't say

who they were fighting with. I heard someone in the pub –
I can't remember who – say there were the McGinleys, at it
again.'

Monaghan stared.

'You couldn't say who they were fighting with? Even
though we have witnesses who put you at the scene when
the fight took place?'

'I've said I was there. I don't know who the other people
involved were. Were some of them men who have worked
for my dad at one time or another? I've no way of knowing.
My dad has some land and whoever works on it is his business, not mine. It's a long time since I've been at home. I'm
not involved in my dad's business.'

Was that just a flicker of a smile on Frank's face?

I leaned back against the mantelpiece, fished cigarettes
and matches from my pockets, and lit up. I inhaled deeply,
and relaxed.

'Why have you been away from home for so long, Mr
O'Reilly?'

'I didn't like walking around my hometown, having
British soldiers and policemen pointing guns at me from
behind every corner. So I left.'

Monaghan grimaced. The cops were silent. I knew now
how powerless they were. The questions went on, but I no
longer listened. This, then, was the pattern of 'routine
enquiries' which you heard so much about.

There was nothing the cops could do.

The notebook was put away.

'Is that everything?'

'Almost. Lads, you can leave.'

The younger officers exchanged a glance, and left the room.

'Should I see your sergeants out?'

'I won't be a minute, Mrs O'Reilly. The formal interview is over. As expected, your alibis have been established. I've no doubt whatsoever that they will check out. What I want to say before we all take our leave is strictly off the record.'

'Hurry up to fuck, then,' Frank said. 'I have work to do, even if you don't.'

I crushed my cigarette out in the cut-glass ashtray on the mantelpiece, and lit another as Monaghan continued.

'You may think you're rebels. You may think you own this town, and that you have the borderlands all sewn up, and that you're beyond the law. You're not. That man suffered before your men blew his brains out, and why? Did you really need the money he was costing you? It's not even your money to begin with, is it? You know what you are? Not heroes. Not outlaws. Not shit-hot gangsters playing by your own rules. You're just common criminals with a wider network of scum working for you, and you know what that means?'

'Enlighten us. You're on a roll.'

'It means you've got more potential weak spots than you can manage. Sooner or later, one of your little rats is going to turn his fucking tail and squeal.'

Outside, an engine revved. Sunlight glared off the glass framing one of the watercolours, making it look blank white. I inhaled two lungfuls of smoke, and held them, where it burned.

'We'll get you. Eventually, we'll get you.'

'I don't care much for your tone.'

'I don't much care what you care for. Goodbye.'

'I'll show you to the door,' Dolores said, rising from the sofa.

Frank grabbed the remote control and flicked on the telly. I watched as the cop cars turned one by one and glided from view, as Frank flicked through the channels. Dolores stood by the front door until the cars vanished, pressed the button that closed the gates, and disappeared into the house, humming to herself.

I followed her into the kitchen.

'That wasn't so terrible, was it? They don't have a leg to stand on, although I do wish your father would show some diplomacy. Still, it's not in his nature, is it?'

I sat down at the breakfast bar.

'Why did you marry him?'

Dolores made a great show of carrying the kettle to the sink, filling it with water, firmly smacking the lid into place, and carrying it back to the base upon which it would boil.

'Drat these kettles, they always go wonky after six months. You'd think I'd learn, wouldn't you? I mean, the French just heat water on the hob. Very sensible. What did you say, darling?'

'Why did you marry him?'

Dolores put her head to one side, tucked a strand of hair behind her ear, and stared at me. She was a good-looking woman. From what I could gather from old photos and the way my various relatives spoke about her, she had always been a good-looking woman, and had had no qualms about using her looks to their full effect. She loved having her picture taken, and looked good in every snapshot, surrounded by all the dullards and fatties. Other people smiled and revealed snaggleteeth or triple chins or webs of wrinkles around the eyes.

When Dolores smiled, the camera smiled back, and there she was, beaming forever in celluloid, making those around her look plain and awkward. Even the fashions of the day flattered her, rather than making her look odd, like they did with most other people. It was there in the feline grace with which she crossed a room, or picked up a magazine, or regarded her reflection with a critical moue in the mirror.

I remembered how once she had drawn Scarlett aside at a very dull family gathering when we were awkward teenagers. My tie had been itchy. Scarlett had been scratching her knees where her tights were wrinkled and beginning to ladder. We were both slumped in a corner sucking on lemonade and wishing that all the ancient, boring people would shut up so they could all go home. Dolores had swept down upon us with a gracious smile.

'You aren't making very good impressions, are you?'

'Sorry, mum.'

Dolores had ignored me, and put her arm around my cousin.

'If you act gorgeous, darling, people believe it.'

Perhaps Scarlett had never believed it.

Just when I was sure that Dolores was going to continue chattering about kettles, she slid onto the seat opposite me, and spoke as if letting me in on a secret.

'Your father is a very ordinary man, in most ways. He was never handsome. He was clever enough, but not especially clever. He wasn't even charismatic, like that red-haired gypsy

Flynn Furey, who had more women running after him than you'd believe. But he did have one thing the other men in this town never had.'

'What was that?'

'Power. You could feel it coming off his skin, like electricity. Oh, I expect that sounds silly to you, but think what it was like for a girl in the '60s in a godawful little town in the North. You had priests and nuns breathing down your neck, quite literally, if you were unlucky enough. No prospects of a decent education, not if you were Catholic, anyway. And you lived at home, more often than not, even if you did get yourself a respectable little job as a secretary, or something. It was stifling. And then into the middle of all the drudgery and duty and abject bloody misery wades this bull of a man who's not afraid to make people angry, or to take what he wants and make no apologies for it. I swooned. I really did. He could have thrown me over his shoulder and carried me off to the mountains, for all I cared.'

'And then?'

'And then marriage. That's how society gets you in the end. For all your dreams and ideals, you become one of them, don't you? Well, you wouldn't know, and good for you, I suppose. Although if you ever did want to get—'

'Mum.'

'I'm sorry, darling, but one does worry about the lame ducks. Where was I?'

'Married.'

'Yes. I mean, your father was a very good provider, and of course business flourished, despite the Troubles. But the power thickened him, the more he got. He coarsened. I expect the work took its toll. You can't look brutality in the face every day and come home with a spring in your step and a heart full of joy because the buttercups are in bloom, can you? No. You can't.'

'He was never violent at home.'

'Oh, no. Just absent. More so, as the years went on.'

The kettle came to the boil, blowing a head of steam into the air, and clicking off.

'Still, never mind,' Dolores said, reaching across the counter to hold my face in her hands. 'If we 'd never married, you wouldn't be you, now would you?'

'Probably not.'

Dolores patted my face, and rose to make the tea.

No matter how much you fantasise that you're a unique human being, an alien dropped into this world, displaced in time and space, suffering the hand you're dealt by fate in terms of family, ability, and prospects, the truth is we're all the simple binary products of our parents' unions, half, more or less, of each one, and never as different from them as we might like to be. Dolores liberally sugared a scalding cup of black tea, and sipped it with a sigh.

'So, mum?'

'Yes?'

'If something happened to Dad—if the cops did catch him—'

'Oh, don't worry about that. I have everything taken care of. If, Heaven forbid, anything happens to your father, we're both well looked after. In fact, in some ways . . .'

A great roar rumbled from the drawing room, as Frank hurled abuse at the TV.

'What?'

'Oh, nothing. Do you want some tea? You did very well

with the police, but you look a bit pale.'

I shook my head, then went back upstairs and lay down on my bed, with my hands behind my head.

It was impossible to keep my mind blank.

The trouble was, a part of me agreed with Chief Superintendent James Monaghan.

9

Graveyard

Every day felt like a fresh slap in the face. Some people greet each morning like a friend, throwing themselves into the day with enthusiasm and joy. People like that are mystifying and enviable.

Other people look upon the morning as an enemy, to be battled with and overcome by perseverance, bloody-mindedness, and the comforting rituals of showering, getting dressed, and coffee, which are more of a psychological crutch than a human necessities. These folk are the majority tribe, ploughing through their day with determination, goals set and small rewards in sight, like a cigarette break at noon, a gossip with a friend at lunchtime, or a bottle of wine at home when the day's work was done.

I sometimes wonder if there are other people like me, people to whom waking up is an unwelcome jerk back into a reality over which they feel no control. Drifting through dreamtime has its appeal. You escape into a fantasy world. Nothing you feel is real. Nothing you do has any consequence. Waking up and facing the world, that's the killer.

I struggled to explain it to myself, never mind anyone else.

'So what are you, a robot?'

'You're a ghost?'

'No, wait, are you one of those people who think you're alive, but everyone else is dead?'

I didn't really think any of those things.

'Maybe you're depressed.'

'Have you thought about taking up jogging?'

'Quit the smokes, man. You'll feel so much better.'

I never took anyone's advice. Who does? You make your own mistakes, and you live with them, until you can't live with them any longer, and something in you snaps.

In the meantime, my brain guided my body through the day-to-day business of being human. Maybe the difference between me and everybody else was I didn't see my own life as a continuous journey, a narrative charting my progress, an adventure starring me as the hero, gaining success against the odds.

It's tempting to construct the story of your life that way, but I don't believe in it. Some people prefer to chart their failure and downfall, but I don't believe in that either. I don't dwell on the day gone by every night before I fall asleep if I can help it. I try not to think too far ahead, or imagine where I might be in one year's time, or five years, or ten years. I'm usually content to roll in and out of bed, taking each day as it comes, living in the moment. Once you remove the planning, scheming, and worry from your day, it keeps you on an even keel, even if that even keel is taking you nowhere much.

But things were beginning to change.

The sun blanched the sky. The hint of showers shadowed the underbelly of clouds. I shoved my hands deep into my pockets and tucked my chin in against the elements. It looked like rain, but I didn't care. I walked through town by myself, because, for once, I needed to time to think.

The houses were conspicuously tidy and clean. No graffiti swore at me from walls. No litter danced at my feet. The kids on the corners left me alone.

I came to the church. The gates were open during the day. I went through, and, as always, felt something of the magic of stepping into a supposedly holy place, which I put down to the sense of silence and devotion you feel for the grand architectural flourishes of the building, and a natural respect for the resting place of the dead.

I walked through the graveyard.

Ironically, it was a good place to be by yourself.

I chose a tree, hitched myself up onto one of the lower branches, and clambered up further, onto a higher branch. I sat with my back against the trunk, legs splayed.

Light appeared dappled through the green-and-gold leaves. I reached for my cigarettes, dropped the packet, swore, looked down to where they had fallen into the mulch below, sighed, leaned back, and closed my eyes.

I thought about Scarlett, trapped in a loveless engagement, and helpless to escape.

I thought about Alison, who depended on her, and Pearse Mahon, who held them both captive and could easily ruin their lives.

I thought about the McGinley brothers, two stupid little wretches who had got in over their heads in a business they didn't understand.

I thought about their murdered father, who should've known what he was letting himself in for, but had let greed blind him to the ruthlessness of the organisation he was pitching himself against.

I thought about the town I'd grown up in, a shrapnel-strewn town set in a lush countryside, and about how a band of rebels had flourished there because of their ideals.

I thought about Duncan, who'd embraced the family business, taken what he could get while it was going, and pissed it up against a wall, and all for nothing.

I thought about Martin, and how much this town had changed, in that someone like him could live proudly and openly, and that cheered me up.

Lastly, I thought about my dad, and wondered if there was anyone alive who could bring about his downfall. The cops couldn't touch Frank O'Reilly.

If he was a monster, then the whole town was gripped in the stranglehold of his empire. If you wanted to make money, you joined O'Reilly's gang. If you needed a favour doing, O'Reilly could arrange it, for a price. If you wanted to earn an honest crust, fair enough, but you'd never compete with the money his cronies had to throw around. They had property, businesses, and land all sewn up. Sooner or later, your money went back to him, didn't it? And if you dared to step on his toes, you were a goner.

By killing McGinley, Frank O'Reilly had shown everyone – friends, neighbours, colleagues, the establishment, and family – that he was the law in his little world.

Was it possible to put a stop to him?

I swung down out of the tree, stamping my cigarettes into the mud.

Now was as good a time as any to quit.

The hedges had recently been hacked down to size, stark and stunted against the lush green fields beyond. Cattle grazed in the fields beyond, staring at me with amiable curiosity for a few moments, before returning to the grass.

Two mares galloped past, hides glossy across taut muscle, manes flickering in the breeze. A car sped past, tooting its horn.

The earth on Duncan's grave was damp and packed in, more like mud than soil. It had rained that morning, and water clung to the branches of trees and blades of grass in the graveyard, beading real flowers and silk ones alike with luminescent pearls of moisture. Rainwater had seeped into the stones, turning them from off-white to ash grey, or ash grey to near black, making almost iridescent the slime of green moss slicked across the older graves. The plots ran down the hillside that the church sat atop, giving a higgledy-piggledy air to the order in which graves ran. Most of the older graves, the ones on the inside of the various pathways, could only be visited by tiptoeing precariously on the stone or marble edges of the surrounding graves.

It was impolite, somehow, to just stride across the marble chips of other people's memories to reach your own loved one's final destination. A few of the graves were little more than scrubby plots of grass, some unremembered, some unmarked, and all that was left of whomever had long since rotted below the small, square patches of struggling greenery, clipped, as duty demanded, by families of their neighbouring dead.

The smell of greenery and wood was everywhere.

The sound of schoolchildren played in the background, trickling like a half-heard melody through my ears.

It was an ethereal place, the swooning branches above the muddy pathways, vast marble statues of angels, a lake of bluebells at the right time of year, an open field sheltered on either side by roads with wooded glades. It felt like a place that existed only for you while you were there. It was possible to meet people also walking through the graveyard or the woods, but by and large, you left each other alone.

Was there a caretaker who kept an eye on overgrown plots?

I stood at the foot of Duncan's grave and looked at the mud, wondering what sort of a headstone Aunty Kate would choose for it, once the customary year had passed in which the grave was left to settle. I got down on my hunkers and picked up a clump of dirt from the grave. I crumbled it between my fingers. Smelled it. Dirt. Just dirt. God, I hoped that Aunty Kate didn't go for one of those headstones with a photo embedded in the middle, or a verse picked out in gold.

Bling bling, you're dead.

I stood up and scanned the graveyard, noting some of the more horrific attempts at memorials.

Weeping angels. Colour photos of the dead, with bad haircuts and out-of-date clothes. Turquoise stones. Some people couldn't even die in good taste.

Although it was early, I was not the only person in the graveyard. A middle-aged man, dapper and well-groomed, laid a bouquet of flowers on a grave with several names etched on the headstone.

Wife? Parents? Children?

The man bowed his head, stood in silence, then crossed himself, but did not leave.

On the far side, a mother pushed a pushchair laden with a wreath and a squirming child from the car park to a grave halfway up the steep incline. She struggled to unstrap the child without losing the pushchair to the force of gravity, jamming a foot under its wheel as both child and wreath were gathered up in arms.

The mother repositioned the pushchair with its front wheel biting the raised stone edge of the nearest grave to the pathway. She tiptoed three graves in, laid the wreath, and pointed at the headstone for the benefit of her child.

The child didn't understand, and didn't care.

Nearby, an elderly woman was ensconced on a collapsible chair, while a capable sort, probably her daughter, weeded the grave they were both perched upon.

'Them roses look lovely.'

'They're carnations, ma.'

'I meant on that other grave over there.'

'Aye, well, carnations were da's favourite, weren't they?'

'Not the point, is it? People think you're cheap if you buy carnations.'

'Who thinks that, exactly?'

'People do. I know what people are like.'

'Da's grave is clean and tidy, ma, that's what people notice.'

'Not half.'

The daughter plucked a stubborn weed up by the roots with a satisfied grimace.

'I don't want no carnations on this here grave when I'm in it, you hear me?'

'You won't have any say in the matter when you're dead, will you, ma?'

Lastly, a kid with a bike stood still on one of the paths, looking at her shoes while an older kid crossed himself at a flower-laden grave. An anniversary, maybe. The older kid turned at the same time as the middle-aged man. They caught each other's eye and nodded, walking off slowly in opposite directions, the middle-aged man alone, the teenager with his arm around his sister.

I coughed up a gobbet of phlegm and spat it out over my shoulder and onto the path, where it quivered for a moment, then sat there, glistening sickly in the sun.

At home, there were things to do. I rang my supervisor at uni and my boss at the bar to let them know I'd be out of action for another couple of weeks. People don't argue with bereavement.

Two weeks.

Two weeks to quit the smokes, lose a van, and disappear.

Dolores didn't understand.

'You're quitting smoking,' she said. 'What for? It's your only pleasure in life.'

'I want to get fitter.'

'Well, I think you're mad. Smoking is what separates us from animals. It's a scientific fact that we're the only species who cooks, and that includes setting fire to leaves. Yes, yes, it's wrong, but that makes it more delicious. Look at all those po-faced little freaks, pinching their noses and spluttering if so much as a whiff of smoke dares whisper across the vapour of their peppermint tea. Please don't tell me you're going to turn into an evangelical anti-smoker, darling. I can't bear anti-smokers, or vegetarians, or born-again lesbians and people like that. So dreary.'

'Thanks. Where can I find Pearse Mahon?'

Dolores sighed.

'Well. It's your funeral, I suppose.'

It felt like it. I finally took that advice and started jogging, partly to get fitter, partly to kill time, and partly to help focus my mind. It was good. It got me out of the house. I saw things in town that otherwise would've passed me by.

My daily route took me past the cattle and sheep in the fields between my house and town. Farmers drove their livestock from pen to grazing ground with tractors, or boys with sticks, or both. It was a reassuringly pastoral sight, compared to the used condoms, drunken homeless folk, and fresh graffiti that greeted me every day in Dublin.

I smelled grass and hay and manure rather than puke and piss and human shit from where junkies used alleyways as places to unleash their bodily waste before shooting up and passing out.

When I'd first moved to Dublin, the amount of human misery stalking the streets in openly smacked out decrepitude had upset me. There had always been a greater gap between the rich and the poor in Dublin than the rest of Ireland, and seeing that gap illustrated in real lives, on a constant basis, was shocking.

At home, benefits were largely something you used to top up your income. In Dublin, people relied on them. Grey-faced stutterers, supermarket shoplifters, and street-corner stalkers bobbed and limped and strutted around in leisure-worn poverty. You couldn't walk the length of one street without someone begging for change, and within one month you'd heard every hard luck story there was – the girl who needed twenty cents for the bus, the bloke who was only asking for a euro for a hostel, the innocent tourist who'd been robbed straight off the ferry and only wanted enough change to make a phone call. I'd soon become sick of the lot of them, yelling at them in my head to get a fucking job, or find some fucking dignity, or get out of my way.

I'd almost forgotten that life in Ireland, outside of that shithole Dublin, was an overwhelmingly rural affair. Farmers still tilled the earth and ran their livestock to and fro, despite diminishing returns. Families lived in houses not surrounded by students and tourists and vagrants, but neighbours, most of whom they knew well, all of whom they knew of.

And when all the kids in a given area went to the same school, the differences between those who had a bit of money, and those who didn't, somehow never mattered as much. It was far from idyllic, but the culture of povvos and poshos was so far submerged in the fabric of everyday life that it scarcely counted.

Money or not, we were only Nordies. But even then, there were little local pockets – like here, in Crossmaglen – where men like my dad came along and skewed the odds. That was when money mattered.

My limbs groaned.

My chest burned.

I told myself to keep on going.

Jog on.

I drank more coffee, which my guts didn't thank me for. I stocked up on chewing gum, to give my mouth something to do when I wanted a smoke. I took up wanking with a resolve unmatched since the last time I'd occupied my teenage bedroom. The physical distractions worked, up to a point. As long as I was doing something, the nicotine cravings were controllable, easy to quash. It was the bouts of pacing the floor, or drumming my fingers while not really watching the telly, or finding myself tossing a book across the room because I needed a smoke, that really began to crack me up.

Jog on.

I stretched, swung my arms, coughed up another load of phlegm, and popped some gum into my mouth. I was doing well. I was in control of my body. I could keep my thoughts and actions focused.

I zipped my hoody up tighter and ran through the grave-yard. All the dead people slept beneath my feet, and the living who loved them came to visit. It was kind of nice, the way people took time out of their day to stop and chat with the dead. I don't think death has to be tragic. Life is the search for something meaningful, not a purposeless scrabble for survival. Some people find meaning in religion, and good luck to them, as long as they don't blow up my train carriage. Some people turn to art, which doesn't do it for me, but it's relatively harmless. Some people look to science, attempting to measure the meaning of life and cross-reference the answers, but until we come up with that unifying theory of everything, it's all good. You choose your side. You make your own meaning.

And as for the meaning of my life, well, I was working on that.

Maybe, if I could upset the balance of power my dad had built for himself, if I could make amends for what he'd done to our community, I'd be able to make a real life for myself, at last.

Jog on.

My feet slapped on the wet concrete path. My footfall echoed off the headstones, sounding flat and hollow. I ran through the piles of dead flesh and bone, the layers upon layers of worm food, or ancestry, or history, or whatever you chose to call the mounds of mouldering carcasses upon which the church stood proudly sentinel. I ran through the trees and shrubbery fed by those lay beneath them, through the stone monuments carved with their stark names and dates, through the plastic flowers and marble memorials, all of which were veined and cold, imitations of life. I ran through the mourners with my jaw set, staring straight ahead, blinking only to wipe the sweat from my eyes. I left them all behind, the living and the dead, determined to take control of what happened next, of the world I'd found myself a part of, of my own as-yet-unlived existence.

10

Easy

Martin and I went for a walk in the countryside. The sun was loving everything real hard. Sweat glistened on our upper lips. Bottles of beer clunked in our backpacks.

'Why's it called John Easy's Hill, do you think?'

Martin pronounced it the Crossmaglen way, 'Asey'. It was impossible not to.

'I suppose John Easy must've lived here once. Or owned the land.'

'But what makes him so special he gets a whole hill named after him?'

'Dunno.'

'Can't be his real name, either. I've never heard of anyone else called "Easy" in these parts. Must've been a nickname. Wonder what it meant.'

'Slutty?'

'You wouldn't say that about a man.'

'Free and easy?'

'Maybe.'

'Laid-back, lazy, easy-going sort of fella, I reckon.'

'So how did he get himself a frigging hill then?'

'You're just jealous. You want a hill named after you.'

'A road.'

'An estate.'

'A town. With a statue, damn it.'

'A five-foot statue? More like a hat-stand.'

'Shut it, fatso.'

'Oi, I've taken up jogging, thanks very much. I look like a pin-up in one of your fag mags, under this T-shirt.'

Martin punched me in the stomach, and I laughed, taking that as my victory.

John Easy's Hill was a steep one, falling from the edge of town and into the fields, hedges and country lanes surrounding it. Daisies, buttercups and dandelions were in bloom by the roadside. The occasional house sat back from the roadside with a smile on its face. The trees were wild but not untamed. It was a quiet, pleasant place to walk, provided you kept an ear out for cars and lorries coming roaring out of nowhere.

'I haven't seen a lot of cops since I've been home. I mean, they called up to the house alright, after the murder, to question us. But you don't see them crawling the streets like you used to.'

'No, that's true.'

'They're everywhere in Dublin.'

'Don't I know it?'

'Not a fan since they beat you up?'

'Never was.'

We walked on.

'I remember falling off my bike as a kid on this hill,' Martin said. 'My mum was taking us out for a spin, we were all geared up for it. Got two minutes down the road after waving to all the neighbours and stuff, and I ploughed head first into the fucking ditch. Arse over tit. Splat. My mum had to pick me up and get me to stop crying and walk us both back home.'

'Were you badly hurt?'

'Nah. I was shaken up, yeah, and I had a black eye, but so what? I should've picked myself up and got on with it, but I was too much of a sissy.'

'You were only a kid.'

'It must have been harsh on my mum, trailing her sissy kid home with a black eye, crying all over the place.'

'Did she ever make you feel that way?'

'Nah.'

'Lucky you, then.'

We took a right down the Lisseraw Road. A horse whinnied at us. I crossed the road, tore up a clump of grass, and held my palm out to the horse, which, after a second's pause, began to nibble at it.

'Good girl.'

I patted the horse's face, and said goodbye to my new friend. Martin had already walked ahead, hands in pockets, squinting up at the sun.

'I'm doing it,' I said.

'Good for you.'

'I mean it. I'm really doing it. I've told my dad I'll do that job for him. I've already made it through an interrogation by the cops. I've kept my mouth shut. I'm doing it.'

'Can you smell the money?'

'Almost. But I'm going one better.'

We stood in the ditch, backs to the hedge, as a tractor trundled past. A bearded farmer in a flat cap nodded to us as he went slowly about his business, in rhythm to the cows chewing cud in the fields. We choked on clouds of diesel and pressed ourselves further back into the hedge.

'What do you mean?'

The hedge clawed at our backs, the muck sucked at our feet, and we felt cows' breath on the backs of our necks.

'I mean, I can beat my dad at his own game. What if I could take the money and run, leaving my dad to face up to what he's done to this town?'

'What the fuck?'

'Think about it. I need the money. Fine. I'll take it. But that doesn't mean my dad gets away with murder.'

We clambered out of the hedge as the tractor disappeared around a corner.

'Please tell me you're not going to tell the fucking cops? Fuck's sake Jay, you'll be killed.'

'How stupid do you think I am?'

'Right now? Pretty fucking stupid.'

'Listen, I'll be fine. I've got a plan. No one will get hurt, except Frank O'Reilly.'

'Have you thought this through?'

'Sure I have.'

'I hope you know what you're doing.'

Martin picked up a stick from where it lay broken in the ditch. He brushed some dirt from it, tested its weight, hacked at some grass, and let it fall in line beside him as a walking stick. The smell of earth, fresh with rain, rose around us. Worms wriggled amongst the roots and flowers at the side of the road.

A cow mooed, louder and deeper than I remembered being possible, and several others joined in or replied.

'What do you think cows talk about?'

'They're probably saying, look at the state of those two

eejits, walking around on two legs like they've got some place to be.'

'Tell me your plan.'

I fell in step beside Martin, swinging my arms in time as he marched.

'OK. It's pretty simple. You can't tell anyone.'

'That's cool. I like my kneecaps just fine.'

'Funny. My dad's plan is that I get the van out of the country and sell it in England.'

'OK.'

'But if I get it to England, the chances of it ever being connected to McGinley's murder is slim to none.'

'Which is the whole idea.'

'Right. So if I want my dad brought to justice, then the van has to be found here in Ireland, preferably this side of the border, and linked back to him somehow.'

'How's that going to happen?'

'Easy. I take the van, drive it to the ferry with the money, ditch it, plant something of Dad's in it, then disappear in a hired car.'

'Your dad won't give you the money until you're in England. You'll get the money from the guy you leave the van with.'

'How do you know?'

'Coz that's what anyone would do. You can't give someone money up front for a job they haven't done yet.'

'OK, OK. So, I drive the van over to England, with something incriminating inside. I'm still working on that part. I swap it for the money, then tip off the cops before I disappear.'

Martin groaned.

'Now you're actively tipping the cops off. You're actually phoning them to get your dad arrested. Think, for fuck's sake. He'll fucking kill you. I'm not joking. You'll actually be dead. No more hot dinners. No more riding. No more waking up in the morning and singing in the shower while a cup of tea brews in the kitchen. Bang bang. Bye-bye.'

'So what do I do, genius?'

'You do what you're told.'

'What?'

'You take the van to England, you get your money, and you fuck off, permanently. You don't look back. You don't call the cops. You don't frame your dad. You walk, he walks, you forget it ever happened, you drink cocktails on the beach for the rest of your life, or whatever the hell makes you happy.'

'I can't do that.'

'You have to.'

'I can't.'

'Why not?'

Martin glared at me in silence.

'It's different for you. You're not ordinary.'

'Wow. Thanks.'

'I don't mean that. I mean, you're not average. You're not just some Average Joe who was born in Crossmaglen, dragged up in Crossmaglen, went to school in Crossmaglen, met a girl in Crossmaglen, wants to have kids and work and settle down in Crossmaglen. This town, it's not for you. You just happen to be from here. Don't pretend that you feel that your roots are here, or that you want to be a part of life in the town, or that you have any love for the place. People like you don't belong in small towns, anywhere, but imagine you were just that Average Joe, born and bred here. What would you do?'

'Get a trade. Like I did, remember?'

'Trade's dead, Martin. It's a recession. All the young families who got a mortgage in the good times but were relying on the housing market – carpenters, builders, painters and decorators – they're fucked.'

'That's too bad. Not everyone can live in a palace. You can't build houses on every square acre of land. You'll run out of space eventually.'

'Look, that's not my point. My point is, for ordinary folk who just want a house and a couple of kids and a job for life, there's fuck all for them here. You want real money, you work for my dad. You aren't faced with that choice.'

'Oh, bollocks. Who doesn't want a house and a marriage and kids?'

'You don't, do you?'

'I might.'

'Well, never mind you. This is about people who have no choice.'

'If you're saying being gay is a choice, I'll batter you.'

'You know what I mean.'

'I wouldn't be so stupid as to put a load of borrowed money into a massive house I mightn't be able to afford in five years' time. I want the same things as everybody else, and I'm not that different from them either. I don't know what you're shiting on about, to be honest.'

'I'm talking about people who don't have the luxury of choice. They're not brilliant, or talented, or creative, or rich. They just want to get by. And if they're from Crossmaglen, what choices do they have? Their best bet is to break the law. That means getting up to their necks in it with my dad. And now my dad has started killing people, and it's not right. It's not cops and robbers any more. Someone died, and I'm not going to let him get away with it. Because if the whole town is in the grip of one murderer, everyone's fucked. Have you forgotten what it was like the last time this town fell into the hands of people with guns?'

'No.'

'Then don't fucking tell me to look the other way.'

Martin chopped at stray branches. I spat, and needed a cigarette.

'You're going to have to be smarter about it,' Martin said.

'What would you do?'

Chop. Whack. Poke.

'You have to assume you'll get the money after you deliver the van, right? So you need to drive the van to England. You also have to assume that unless the van is found here, near enough to town, it's not going to be connected to the McGinley murder. Which means you also need to abandon the van here, before you take the ferry.'

'My head hurts.'

'It'll hurt a lot more if it's splattered all over the pavement. You need a second van, dummy. You're going to leave the real van here and drive the substitute van over to England, swap it for the cash, and disappear.'

'I am?'

'Yeah.'

'That'll work?'

'You've got to hope that the real van isn't discovered before you swap the fake van for the money. If it's found, you're dead.'

'You can help me with that.'

'How?'

'What if you phoned the cops about the van after I get the money?'

'No way. I'm not getting involved. I'm definitely not calling the cops. Anyway, think about it. Me calling them doesn't mean the van won't be found before the phone call.'

'True.'

'I'll tell you what, though. If the real van is found, I'll text you, how about that? You'll have time to fuck off, but you'll have to forfeit the money.'

Yeah. If the van was found abandoned, my dad would know I'd betrayed him. And if he knew that, he'd pick up the phone and make sure someone in England found me and put a bullet in my head. Being his son wouldn't matter anymore. I wanted the money, sure, but I'd live without it, if I had to.

'Fair enough,' I said.

'Good. Now, where are you going to get the second van?'

'I've an idea about that.'

'Don't tell me.'

Clouds swabbed out the sun. A breeze rustled through the brittle branches of the hedges, clicking them against each other like a miniature round of applause. A fox peered out from under a bush, spiked us with its yellow eyes, and dashed away.

'Oh, I was thinking some more about what you said in the café. That thing about how to disappear completely,' Martin said.

'Yeah?'

'I know how I'd do it.'

'Yeah?'

'Yeah. Find someone about the same height and build. Seduce him with my manly charms. Then I'd kill him, right, take his credit card and passport, and book a flight for the next day in his name. Then I'd put him in my clothes with some of my stuff lying around, put him in an old house, set fire to the lot, and vamoose, passing myself off as him. Pretty clever, huh? He'd have to be ginger, just in case. But no one would suspect the dead body wasn't me, so a little discrepancy over height or teeth or whatever wouldn't be questioned.'

'I was wrong about you. You're an evil genius. Why are you helping me?'

'Coz you'd be dead if I didn't.'

'Yeah, but so what?'

Martin threw the walking stick back into the ditch.

'I owe you one.'

'Do you?'

'Yeah.'

'Why?'

'For that time on the square.'

'That wasn't a big deal.'

'It was a pretty big deal to me.'

The countryside was not silent. The burr of tractors, the lowing of cows, and the occasional yap of a dog were strung through the air, but serenity stretched for miles in every direction. We stopped amid acres of green, topped with a bright blue sky, spun through with white clouds. It seemed like a place where nothing bad could happen. we'd said enough. we'd come to a quiet spot that used to be a handball alley. We didn't want to use the handball alley itself, as the tall concrete walls would make echoes for a mile or so around.

The tall walls would make for good cover, though.

There was no one else around. Martin set up the tin cans and bottles on the edge of a fence, and I pressed six bullets into the handgun. Martin set them up in perfect alignment, two feet apart, then scurried out of the way as I squinted down the barrel of the gun. The targets glinted in the sun, glass and metal gleaming like trinkets in a shop window. I lay flat in the grass a couple of hundred yards away from the fence, and trained my eye to pick out the tiny victims waiting in a line for me to blow them all to pieces.

Martin flopped down beside me in the grass.

His breathing was slow and heavy. His sweat smelled like summer. The sun bounced off his copper locks, white skin turning pink in the heat. I wriggled on my belly, ignoring a bead of sweat that dripped from temple to my jaw.

You had to forget the distractions, the sweat, the arm hair tickled by the grass, the insects buzzing by your face. You had to let your breathing slow down to the same tempo as the lad beside you, so that you both melted into the ground – an extension of the land, that's all you were.

You had to hold your hands steady, as your thumb rubbed over the safety catch, and your grip on the barrel tightened, and your trigger finger squeezed down gently.

The glass bottle shattered, casting a million points of light through the air, raining shards. The bang of the gun lived barely as long as the splinters of glass. Deep silence.

'Again,' Martin said.

I picked off the targets one by one – glass shattering, tin splattering, and the fence splintering when I nicked it with a stray shot. When we got up from the grass, our jeans and T-shirts were drenched in sweat. We clinked a couple of beers and lay back to bask in the sun. It felt good, to have a purpose in life.

Martin flicked the sweat out of his fringe and rubbed his face with the edge of his T-shirt, exposing a fiery trail of copper crawling up his belly. I enjoyed the cool fizzle of the beer on my tongue and the back of my throat, bubbles evaporating like the sweat on my back, the way love does in the harsh light of day.

Nobody would miss me that much when I disappeared.

'It was a Saturday, two weeks before my Confirmation,' Martin said. 'My head was full of prayers, when to stand, when to kneel, when to walk to the top of the church. All I wanted was my dad's hand on my shoulder when I received the Holy Spirit into my soul. I was a real Holy Joe, can you believe it? It was only the kids with no imagination who didn't believe in God. I hated the idea of Confession, though. Sitting in a dark box, whispering all your secrets, making things up coz you had to say something. I knew not to let on about wanting to kiss some of the other boys. I always liked the tough ones, even if they called me a faggot and a gyppo. I think everyone's God is just a voice in their head. It's just the part you keep buried, and whether you think God is good or bad depends on your nature.'

'And then what happened?'

'And then the world blew apart.'

We finished our beers. Martin lined up the bottles on the fence.

'Come on. Once more for luck.'

Easy.

11

The Land of Ire

Pearse Mahon worked cash-in-hand at the local garage, thanks to Frank pulling a few strings for him. He was working alone today. I stood across the road. The kids, the shops, the litter, the cars, the pubs, the broken glass, the chipped paint, the Northern Irish sing-song accent, bandit country, a place of unmentionable fury, no man's land.

Ireland, the Land of Ire, I thought, *and nowhere more so than here.*

I had discovered my own well of anger. It was deep in my chest, an anger that Scarlett would never escape this town. An anger that all the local boys looked up to my dad as a role model to emulate or obey. An anger that money, only money, sang to us, myself included, and no one wanted justice any more – we only wanted a slice of what had been denied to us for so long.

I stood there staring across the road, just past the entrance to Scarlett and Pearse's estate. Three fat women out walking for their health scuttled by.

Deep breaths.

The estate was quiet. Most people were either at work, having tea at home in front of the telly, or sleeping off last night's pints before rising in the afternoon. I waited until the waddlers were gone, then turned my back on the town, whipped my cock out over the top of my joggers, and pissed over the fence of the nearest yard.

Bliss. I hoped the flowers didn't mind.

The garage had two petrol pumps and a workshop for MOTs, changing tyres, reupholstering seats, polishing rims, or, if the need arose, spray-painting, changes to the body work, and a swift swap of number plates.

Sure, it was a legitimate business, but that didn't mean Frank couldn't use it to get rid of hot vehicles.

It was time to confront Pearse Mahon.

I steeled myself.

A car came out of nowhere, speeding up the road, bouncing over bumps, its suspension shot. It didn't stop, but roared past, tooting its horn. I took that as a good sign, strode across the road, and walked through the doorway before I could change my mind.

The workshop was small and gloomy. My eyes began to adjust to the shadows as Pearse broke free from the corner, where he'd been tinkering with a car, its maw open, guts in pieces on the floor.

'Jay.'

'Pearse.'

A lamp glowed behind him, yellow light poured upon the inner machinery of the car. I noted the weapons at hand – a spanner, a torch, and a metal face mask, which meant that a blowtorch was lying around somewhere. Pearse wiped his oily hands across the white vest covering his chest. He was wiry, rather than muscular. We were much the same height, but I had the advantage of weight, and preparation.

'Dirty paws. Sorry if I don't shake hands. What can I do for you?'

'You can stop beating the shit out of Scarlett.'

Pearse stopped, blinked, opened his mouth, closed it again, then settled on a smile.

'I don't know what you're on about, buddy.'

'The black eyes. The bruises. The battering she takes from you when you're drunk and pissed off and need to feel like a man.'

Pearse looked around, wiped his hands on his vest again, and shook his head.

'She had a fall, OK? You got it wrong.'

'Bullshit.'

'I'm at work, for fuck's sake. Can't we talk about this later?'

'Quit fucking whining. We're talking about this now.'

'If you—'

'What?'

Pearse snarled and lunged at me with a balled fist. I stepped aside, catching Pearse's fist in mine. I crushed his fingers. Pearse whimpered. Grabbing his other wrist, I wrenched his hands behind his back, holding them tight. There was no struggle. He fell limp in my grip. Like all wife beaters, Pearse Mahon was a coward.

'Do I need to teach you a lesson?'

Pearse said nothing.

'Do I need to break your face across the floor? Split your knees with your own spanner? Snap every bone in your fingers so badly you won't be able to toss off for twelve months?'

'That's what Scarlett's for, isn't it?'

I snatched up the torch and cracked it across Pearse's skull before he had a chance to swing around and disarm me. He fell to the floor, a trickle of blood tracing the line from temple to cheekbone. It dripped onto the concrete as he retched, hands clawing the bare ground. I felt the weight of the torch in my hand and marvelled at what I'd done. So easy to act before you could think, to lash out, and find yourself peering down upon the cut-open heap at your feet.

Pearse scrabbled in the dirt, heaving, catching his breath. He put a hand to his head, looked at his bloody fingertips in disbelief, and groaned.

'Keep your fucking hands off her in future, you hear me?'

Pearse hung his head. Blood wept from his wound, spilling onto the floor like tears from a statue of the Virgin Mary.

Pearse pulled himself up on his knees, as if in prayer.

'You don't know what it's like.'

'What what's like?'

'What it's like to have nothing. Be nothing.'

'What are you on about?'

'Look at this shit,' Pearse said, taking in the room with outstretched hands.

'I tried to work hard, tried to get on, but I'm not that smart. I did my best, but there's always someone quicker, someone better. I was getting by, not brilliantly, like some, but getting by, then – bang. There's no money out there anymore. No one's spending, everybody's shitting it. What am I supposed to do? I take what I can get, that's what. And it fucking kills me. Do you think I want to be this person? Do you think I want to punch the woman I love?'

'Well, you fucking did it, didn't you?'

I tightened my grip on the torch.

'OK, so I'm not bad looking. That's something I've got.

And it got me a woman like Scarlett – beautiful, kind, clever.'

'Too good for you.'

'She is too good for me. I know it. And then I got her pregnant and Alison came along – I love them both, I do – but she's stuck with me now. We've got this baby, this – this life. And I think of what she could've had if she got away before she met me, and sometimes I think she must hate my guts.'

'She doesn't hate you.'

'She should hate me. No real job, no real money, scraping by in a house her family bought for us.'

'You should be grateful they spent the money on you.'

'I want to buy my own house, for just the three of us. I'm not a bad person. I come home after a shitty day, making fuck all, dog tired, half drunk, and the baby's crying and my woman hates me and I can see it, I can see it in her eyes, looking at me like I'm scum, a disappointment, and she's so fucking beautiful I don't deserve to touch her, and . . .'

Pearse slumped to the ground with his face in his hands, sobs wracking his body.

I looked down at him in disgust.

'Quit yapping, for fuck's sake.'

Pearse wiped his face, tears and blood and snot smeared across his good looks.

'I don't give a shit how hard done by you think you are. It doesn't give you the right to raise your hand to a woman, any woman, let alone the mother of your child.'

'I know that.'

'Start fucking believing it.'

Pearse hung his head.

I had a choice. The little wretch was here at my feet, battered, bruised, and ripe for a beating, but also as pathetic as a playground bully spanked by his dad in front of his victims. Despite my better judgment, despite the itching in my fists to do to Pearse what Pearse had done to Scarlett, I felt a knot of something like pity in my throat.

I chucked the torch aside.

'Get up.'

Pearse eyed me suspiciously.

'I'm not going to hit you. Just get to your feet.'

Pearse stood up slowly, watching me for any sudden movements. He pulled up his vest to wipe his face clean. I saw several small, round scars etched into his belly. Cigarette burns from childhood? Maybe. It didn't matter. I looked away as Pearse pulled his face from his vest, righting his stained clothing as best he could.

'If I hear one more whisper that you've laid a hand on Scarlett, you're dead. Got it?'

'I won't.'

'Tell me you've got it.'

'I've got it.'

'Good. Now, this is what you're going to do . . .'

Pearse just stood there looking at the floor as I made my demands. He thought I was mad, but he agreed to everything. I'd taught that bollix a lesson, and I'd got him on my side too. It was a good start, but I couldn't trust him. I needed more leverage, if I was going to use him to overthrow my dad's little empire. I needed an ally he would listen to. I needed him to feel that he had everything to lose, and only I could give him what he wanted.

It felt good, and it was only the beginning. I wanted more.

Two men were fighting outside the chippy, poking each other in the chest. The taller man tapped the other lightly on the face, as if daring him to respond. The shorter man let fly his fists, his lunch falling to the ground. The taller man held the shorter man back at arm's length, a palm on his forehead, laughing as the flying fists fell short of his beer gut.

A cat snuck by and dragged a battered fish from the fallen mound of paper, chips and grease, disappearing as the scrap dissolved into nothing.

A girl with a green balloon stared at the broken window of somebody's home. The cracks in the glass spread like an exploding star across the drab and shabby front of the house. Did she live there? Probably not. There was no sign of life behind the broken glass. A gust of wind jerked the balloon from the girl's hand, and she jumped in vain to catch it as the wind tugged it from her grasp and away, up beyond the telephone wires slung between houses, up towards the clouds, the sky, vast and empty space.

A drunken old man picked a fight with someone who wasn't there. He ranted at the imaginary being by his side, flecks of spittle falling from his lips.

Then he stopped mid-sentence and broke into a chuckle, which rose from his gullet into a full-blown guffaw. He bent double with laughter, slapping his knees in joy at some hilarious figment of his own imagination.

I hadn't felt this alive in a long time, not since Martin and I had been kids, running around causing trouble, making everybody hate us.

Martin had been an altar boy before he'd lost his faith.

We'd ran amok one Christmas, drunk on stolen altar wine, which he'd smuggled out after Midnight Mass. The cheap red wine had stained our lips and teeth black. we'd looked like monsters, passing the bottle between us, slugging something that was more than alcohol but less than the blood of Christ, drunk on our own irreverence as much as the wine.

'Was Jesus a zombie? Think about it. I mean, he came back from the dead, and then started brainwashing everyone.'

'But he wants us to eat him, not the other way round. So are we cannibals, every time we go to Communion?'

'Bit of a death cult, this religion malarkey.'

The priest had spent Midnight Mass giving out about the long-lived pagan rituals which his church had shamelessly co-opted for its own benefit, the brunt of his vitriol aimed at Santa Claus and the commercialisation of the season, which boiled down to grousing about families spending money on presents for each other, instead of giving it to him.

The Christmas tree in the square was lit with gloriously tacky multicoloured lights, like an evergreen conifer in drag. we'd stumbled drunkenly beneath strings of plastic angels, neon slogans lighting up the street, as we'd chased each other through the shrubbery like two of Santa's elves on the lam from his toy factory.

At the bottom of the square, a wooden nativity scene sat in pride of place outside the community centre. The cow and the donkey glared cross-eyed at each other. The Three Wise Men hitched their skirts up as they knelt in the straw, presents presented with girlish curtseys. The Virgin Mary smiled benevolently at the barracks across the road. The trough for the Baby Jesus was empty, awaiting his delivery in the morning, presumably by the Holy Spirit in the guise of a stork.

Martin ran all the way to the manger. I ran after him.

He clambered into the nativity scene, threw himself down in the trough reserved for the Baby Jesus, hoisted his legs up in the air, and pulled down his jeans and his jocks, mooning the whole town with his bare ginger arse.

'I'm the Baby Jesus. Eat me!'

He'd made page five of the local newspaper, which meant he was forever famous in his own postcode area.

I broke into a big, wide grin, and ran all the way to Scarlett's house.

12

Cousins

'What the fuck do you think you're doing?' Scarlett said. 'Who do you think you are? You can't just walk back into a person's life and order them around like you own them.'

I stood there gawping.

Scarlett clutched her hair.

'Can't you just mind your own business?'

This wasn't exactly how I'd imagined it would go.

'Calm down.'

'Why should I? I haven't seen you in, like, three years, and then you come waltzing back and decide what's best for me and Alison? I don't fucking think so, Jay.'

'Let's go to the living room, come on. Sit down. I'll make a cup of tea. You're beginning to sound like an American TV show, for fuck's sake.'

Scarlett stuck out her chin and screwed up her eyes, and I was transported back in time to her old backyard, Scarlett in the sand pit, raising a spade because I'd dared to splash her with water. I giggled.

'I'm serious, damn it.'

'I know, I know. I'm sorry. You just look so—'

'Stay away from Pearse.'

'Just sit down, we can talk about it.'

'Fine. But you're not staying long.'

We went into the living room. Alison was banging on a toy drum with one of her shoes. She gurgled at me and I waggled my fingers at her. Kids turn everyone into morons. Scarlett perched on the arm of a chair.

'Stay. Away. From. Pearse.'

'I was only trying to help.'

'I don't need your help. I know what sort of a man he is, and most of the time he's a good one.'

'And the rest of the time?'

'The rest of the time is none of your business.'

'Bullshit. We're family.'

'Yeah, and in a week's time you'll be gone again, and I won't see you for another three years.'

'I'll probably be gone a lot longer than that. Maybe for good.'

'Well, there you go, then. What use are you going to be to me, when you're off in Dublin or London or New York, or wherever you're going to next? I'm the one who has to stay here and live. It's *my* life, Jay, *my* life, and you don't have the right to poke your nose in and then disappear.'

'You're right. I'm sorry.'

That took her by surprise. She looked confused.

'Oh.'

Scarlett stood up, hesitated, and sat down again.

'It's just that . . . You don't know what sort of a life he's had.'

'That's true.'

'It was tough for him,' Scarlett said, her fingers making knots in her lap. 'His dad was a bastard. He used to beat the shit out of him, told him he was good for nothing. He's got scars from where his dad stubbed cigarettes out on his chest.'

'That's awful.'

'Another time, his broke three bones in Pearse's foot from stomping on them so hard. His dad was jealous that Pearse spent so much time at football training. He put Pearse's own boots on and went to town on his foot, studs and all. Can you imagine?'

'I didn't know that.'

'How could you? Pearse had to give up football. Before that, he wanted to play professionally. Maybe he never would've made it, but he never got the chance to try. I know it's not an excuse for some of the things he's done, but it's a reason.'

'Not a very good one, Scarlett.'

'No, maybe not. But he tries to be a better man than his dad. How many abused kids can say that?'

'I don't know.'

'I know he's got his problems, Jay, but I love him all the same. I love him.'

You can't argue with love. Poets weep, artists mourn, singers descend into a drug-fuelled hell, and love lives on. No one ever pays attention to the warning signs. They blindly go looking for love again, and getting their hearts broken. I've never been in love, not really, and no one's ever loved me blindly, not that I know of, anyway.

I wonder what it's like. Exhausting, probably.

'Sorry if I upset you, Scarlett.'

'Da, da, da,' said Alison.

The living room was artificial, ugly and boring, nothing more than the replication of an advert in a magazine, utterly soulless. So many people put their hopes and dreams into marriage, babies, and a home. It was my idea of hell, but this was everything Scarlett wanted.

If I gave her the option, would she run away and start a new life, or stay where she was, and pour all her money and love into propping up the dream with Pearse Mahon?

I could only give her the choice, but what she did with it was up to her.

'So,' Scarlett said, sitting beside Alison on the floor, playing with her hair. 'What else have you been up to?'

'Hanging out with Martin Furey.'

'Are you going to run away together and live in a caravan?'

'Very funny. We're just mates. We were both there when that lorry launched a mortar attack on the army base, way back when. Remember?'

'Oh yeah, I remember. You came home with blood all over you, acting as if nothing happened.'

'Did I?'

'You did. You came round to our house after it happened, remember?'

'That's right.'

'We had just got up off the floor and put the radio on, and you strolled in with blood on your hands, and we all thought you'd helped a dying soldier by the roadside, or something. That's the sort of stupid thing you would've done too, you eejit.'

'It was Martin's blood. He was just a kid. He cut his knees when he fell off his bike. He almost ran into the middle of it all, just before the soldiers started shooting back at the lorry. You don't think about it, do you, when you're young?

It's just part of life, like school, or having to brush your teeth, or the electricity cutting out during a storm and having to walk around with candles. There were all these murders happening on our doorstep. You just get used to it.

'That's life, isn't it?'

'Tragic and meaningless?'

'Stuff that happens around you, and you take it for granted.'

'Well, I'd better go,' I said.

'Look, about the money,' Scarlett said.

'About the money,' I said. 'I'll give you half it, but it depends on Pearse's help. It's a simple thing. No one's going to get hurt, I promise. One job, and the money's mine. You need it as much as I do. You'll take fifty grand, no questions asked, won't you?'

Scarlett frowned.

'What's the catch?'

'No catch. The risk is all mine, and it's a small one.'

'And Pearse has agreed to help you? First you threaten him, then you attack him, and now you want his help?'

'Think of the money. He is. We can do this, but you've got to trust me. Please.'

'Fifty grand?'

I nodded.

'I'm listening,' Scarlett said, picking Alison up from the floor, ignoring her protests as she sat on the sofa, gently bouncing her daughter on her knee. Her eyes were wary.

I sat beside her.

'I need Pearse to get me a van. A white van. If I get him the make and model and number plates, he can do that for me, right? He said he could. I'm relying on him, but I need you to work on him too. Don't let him fuck this up for us. Tell him I've told you what I want. Tell him we've all agreed to do this.'

'Why?'

'I can't tell you why. Trust me.'

'Jay, is this about . . . ?'

'Never mind what this is about, that part's not important. What is important is getting that van. If we do it, the money's ours, and we're home and dry.'

'I don't understand. If you wanted a van, couldn't Frank . . . ?'

'Frank is testing me. I've got to come through with the van, in the strictest secrecy. Do you understand? Frank can't hear about this, or we're fucked. I'm fucked. But get Pearse to do this one thing for me, and I swear, I'm off his back forever. The money's yours, to do whatever you want with. Save it, spend it, smoke it, I don't care. OK?'

Scarlett was silent for a minute.

'I'll see what I can do,' she said.

I hugged her, a rib-crushing hug that came straight out of childhood.

'You're the best.'

'I can't make any promises.'

'It's going to work, I know it.'

'If you're planning something stupid . . .'

'Of course I'm not. I'm doing this for us.'

'Us,' Scarlett said.

'Meet me tomorrow. Let me know what Pearse says. Tell him I'm sorry about what happened, whatever it takes.'

'Oh. You've just reminded me. You know what day tomorrow is?'

'Barely. Is it important?'

'It's Muck McGinley's funeral.'

'Do you think we should go?'

'Are you mad?'

'Why shouldn't we?'

'You've lost it. I'm seriously worried now.'

'Come on. Frank can't go, fair enough, there'd be riots. But why shouldn't we?'

'As what? The Peace Squad? Extend the olive branch and declare a truce?'

'No. To keep an eye on things. Show our faces. Pay our respects.'

'The cops will be all over it.'

'No law against attending your neighbour's funeral. It might look worse if none of our family showed. You went to school with the twins, didn't you?'

'They were hateful little fuckers then too.'

'Great, so you won't even be upset. We can leave if it gets hairy. Besides, aren't you even a little bit curious?'

Scarlett hesitated.

'Eleven fifteen at the steps of the church, so we don't have to do the procession.'

'It's a date.'

'Some date,' Scarlett said, bashing me over the head with a cushion.

'Another funeral to look forward to. We're so Irish, it hurts.'

'I'll hurt you for real if you fuck this up.'

'I won't. Hey, what's the most Irish thing you can think of?'

'Like what?'

'Like, I don't know. Imagine something that could only

happen in Ireland. OK, here's one I saw on the way to the train station before I came home. A man kneeling in prayer outside Tesco's, protesting about the sale of Israeli blueberries.'

'Oh, good one. How about this? A procession of grannies and foreigners, reciting the Stations of the Cross in the street on Easter weekend.'

'Yeah, cool. Two drunks on the steps of a church, squabbling over the last dribble of Buckfast in their bottle.'

'A homeless, pregnant woman smoking outside Spar, while her boyfriend shits into a plastic bag.'

'A builder eating a breakfast roll in a ghost estate months after everyone else has gone home, in case the investors come back to rob the bricks.'

'An elderly mother and son, picketing a gay pride parade with anti-abortion placards.'

'A priest fiddling a kid in the confession box. That's got to be a classic.'

'Timeless. How about the same kid going on *The Late, Late Show*, promoting his misery memoir, *Touched By An Angel . . . Down There.*'

'His clairvoyant sister writing a sequel, *Angels in My Pubic Hair.*'

'Oh, I've got a good one. This actually happened. A hungover chef in Dublin airport throwing up in a frying-pan while he's making breakfast, and serving it to an American tourist as a Full Irish Omelette.'

'A teenage girl waking up the day after her debs and saying a prayer to St Antony to help find her lost virginity.'

'Wanting to be Catholic, as long as you can practise all the Protestant bits.'

'Cynic. A white guy proving he's not racist by sharing his Bob Marley ringtone with the black toilet attendant in his local pub, then asking if he can score some weed.'

'Two junkies unknowingly re-enacting a scene from Beckett at a bus stop.'

'Claiming you're a feminist on Twitter, but live tweeting the Rose of Tralee.'

'Voting for someone you met at your great-uncle's wake, even though you know he'd rob the brass fittings off the coffin if he got the chance.'

'A woman spending fifty euro on a new hairdo for her wedding anniversary, then wearing a GAA jersey to the local Italian restaurant.'

'Her husband ordering every course on the menu with a side of chips.'

'Prawn cocktail with chips. Ham and pineapple pizza with chips. Tomato, mozzarella and rocket salad with chips.'

'A nurse and a guard getting married after he gets her pregnant in an alleyway, and everyone thinking they're great because they have pensions and a mortgage and didn't get an abortion.'

'Sitting beside the happy couple on Table Seventeen at your second cousin's wedding, being forced to listen to them advise you to go into teaching, because the holidays are great.'

'A finance graduate working for minimum wage in a fast-food restaurant, spitting in everyone's food because there's a moratorium on banking jobs.'

'A seasoned civil servant who turns up for work every day, and then falls asleep at his desk, drooling onto an unread copy of the *Irish Times*.'

'A busker covering the songs of Jeff Buckley and Radiohead, while he considers getting into heroin so he can really feel the pain of the singer-songwriter.'

'A beggar on a street corner, bartering smokes off Romanian kids for copies of his self-published poetry.'

'A former voice actor who made a fortune during the Troubles, swearing at the TV every time he hears Gerry Adams speak.'

'A terrorist freed in the Good Friday agreement, who starts a self-help group for disenfranchised fundamentalists.'

Alison began to cry.

Scarlett stopped laughing and passed the baby over to me. I sniffed her nappy while her mum prepared a bottle. Alison sucked the warm milk, then began to doze off.

No matter how much fun you're having, babies kill it. Yet another thing you can't stop people doing, no matter how badly it tends to turn out. Making love and making babies are nature's biggest gimmicks.

Scarlett put Alison down on a blanket, and we quietly whispered our goodbyes.

'We are so going to hell.'

'It's cool. No one believes in hell anymore.'

Outside, it looked like a storm was brewing. I'm not superstitious, so I didn't read anything into the bruised purple sky, the glowering clouds, the promise of thunder and rain on the horizon. Wherever they hung out these days, God and the Devil were having a good laugh at my expense.

13

Burial

It rained, and made no apology for it. I shivered under an umbrella as sheets of water slashed down from the heavens, falling in almost vertical panes of ice. It stung to the touch. Even standing there at the foot of the church steps, back to the stone wall, I could feel the rain bouncing off my shoes and splattering up my legs and pounding around my ears. I hate metaphorical weather. Why couldn't we have a nice soft day? But no. It was going to be one of those days where you couldn't tell if your toes were really wet, or just numb and cold. I wondered how long Fr Flaherty was going to keep us outside, up to our shins in mud. My knuckles turned blue as I gripped the umbrella tighter. I cursed myself for the bright idea of attending Muck McGinley's funeral at all.

Rain pelted the shop fronts, slathering their windows with a slick sluice of water that was there, gone, there, gone, falling away in an instant, only to be followed by the exact same rain slick again. I stared at the process of rain dashing against a shop front, trying to break the process down into its constituent parts, willing it to go in slow motion so I could measure the way in which water fell, in individual drops and as a body, and then trickled away to nothing, but everything became a blur. I couldn't fool my brain into seeing the rain fall as a camera would.

I blinked. Rain flooded the gutters, saturated granite, flattened grass, battered flowers, bombed homes, zinged off speeding cars, blinded pedestrians, shot cats and dogs so that they ran for shelter, and pissed me off. Spits of rain trickled down the back of my collar. I hunched my shoulders and wished I'd worn a scarf, even if they did look sissy.

Scarlett grabbed my elbow, ducking under the umbrella, and I forgot about my wet neck. She shook her hair like a dog, shivering and stomping her feet, heels clicking on the pavement. I felt a rush of manliness, with the blonde girl clinging to my arm, shield at the ready, head bare to the elements. OK, so it was an umbrella rather than a shield, but still.

'I left Alison at Aunty Kate's. God, what a rotten day.'

'Happy the corpse it rains on.'

'I doubt it. I hope they hurry up, I want to go inside.'

'This must be the first time you've ever been eager to get to church.'

'Do you think we should sneak in?'

'Too late. Here they come.'

The hearse crawled through the rain, trailing its mourners under black umbrellas, the relentless spill of water pouring down without regard for their thin black clothing, sore feet, make-up, hair gel, or feelings. They moved through the rain like a mirage, shimmering, barely real. How stupid, to maintain the brave face of a traditional procession through town with the corpse kept cosy and dry in a wooden box in the back of a big car, while all its living relatives and friends are soaked to the skin for half a mile behind it.

Camera crews circled the bereaved at a barely respectable distance, wires and booms and cables snaking between TV and radio reporters, just visible from where they'd set up camp in the square. Cops were dotted in between the real people. There was Monaghan, speaking into a walkie-talkie, distant, impotent, and faintly ridiculous in the flat navy cap which dripped water onto the end of his long nose.

The immediate family came slowly into focus. There were the twins, there was Mrs McGinley, her brothers and sisters, arms around small children, youngsters blank-faced, elders in tears, leaning against each other as they stumbled through the rain, other mourners following slowly. I swallowed hard, holding Scarlett's arm tighter to my side, staring back at hundreds, thousands, of accusing eyes. Maybe they weren't all looking at me, but it felt like they were. Alerted by a boy on lookout duty, the priest swept into view at the top of the church steps, flanked by three altar boys and an altar girl – even Crossmaglen had to bow to the demands of modernity in some respects. The tallest of the boys held an umbrella over Fr Flaherty's head.

'The church is going to be full.'

'Should we sneak in the side and get a seat?'

'Look, we can't. How would it seem if two O'Reillys snuck in and got seats for the McGinley funeral before the family had a chance to shake out their umbrellas? Jesus, it'd nearly be worse than killing the fella.'

'Oh, all right.'

'I don't think we're going to get a seat. Look at all those people.'

'As long as we're standing out of the rain, I don't care.'

A single bell began to bong its sombre monologue as the hearse drew up to the foot of the church, the undertakers nimbly skipping through the raindrops to slide the coffin out of the car and onto a collapsible trolley, and then swiftly hoist it onto the shoulders of the twins, and two of their cousins. I looked down, down into the swirling gutter, hoping once again that my gaze would pass for reverential prayer, or at least a solemn contemplation of time and its many ravages, but this time, I knew I wasn't fooling anyone. I felt ashamed.

'Come on,' Scarlett whispered, and we slid into the crowd. We joined the procession, climbing up the steep steps of the church, reminded – how could we not be? – of Duncan's funeral, only two short weeks ago. The same steps, the same sad faces, the same shuffle of grief, the same sniffles and weeping, the same dragged-out sense of time in which every minute lasted one whole hour, and every hour was lived as fully as one whole day.

With a glance at each other and a nod of understanding, we took a detour and slipped around to the side entrance of the church. Several dozen other people had had the same idea. Even squeezing in through the side door was a challenge. There was just enough room to stand elbow to elbow by the time the last few people found space. Some poor saps were stuck outside in the rain.

I passed my umbrella to a surprised and grateful woman who was finding it hard to stay dry beneath the inadequate shelter of her enormously fat husband.

'We'll need that later,' Scarlett hissed.

'Nah. The sun will come out in a bit. It always does.'

In the tiny little hallway between the old graveyard and the pews stage-right of the altar, it was difficult to hear any of the ceremony, apart from the pieces performed by the organist and choir. They warbled inharmoniously as friends and family bobbed and bowed and spoke through choked-back tears from the pulpit. The whispers, farts and giggles of the assembled company in the hallway were much more real than the sanctimony of the ceremony.

I dreamt of other things, and stood my ground during Communion, glad of the slight respite offered from the crush of bodies in the hall, as everyone traipsed to the altar to receive the body of Christ, or the magic wafer, whatever you were having yourself.

I think the reason Protestants split from the Holy Catholic Church was largely down to temperament. Catholics were happy to live in poverty and worship in luxury. Protestants wanted it the other way round.

Sure enough, Mass ended, as it had to.

We were in the hallway they had to carry the body through, on the way to the burial. As we shook our dead legs and spilled into the graveyard, the rain ceased abruptly, and the sun broke free from behind a cloud. Golden rays pierced the grey concrete slabs and sparse specks of greenery. Hallelujah.

'Now there's timing for you.'

'Thank God.'

'It's a miracle.'

Arm in arm, we embraced the daylight.

'Will we stay for the burial?'

'From a distance.'

We watched from the top of the graveyard's sloping hill as Muck McGinley's body was lowered into its grave, one twin either side of his mother. She almost collapsed as the priest said yet more magic words, tossing a fistful of dirt on top of the mahogany box.

'Weird.'

'That he's buried right beside Duncan?'

'Yeah.'

'I suppose we'll always have to bring two wreaths to the graveside from now on.'

Water vapour from the concrete path rose in a shimmering haze. The scene below flickered like an old television set. The sudden sun was hot, making my clothes seem twice as damp and sticky. I stuck a finger in my collar and wiggled it around.

'You know what they're doing, don't you?' Scarlett said.

'Who?'

'The twins. They're off to Australia. There's no recession over there, the Aussies love a drink, and they're all descended from criminals. They should fit right in.'

'I hope they get kicked in the nuts by kangaroos.'

Scarlett snorted in laughter. Several dozen pairs of eyes swivelled towards her. She tried to turn her laughter into an approximation of tears, resting her head in the crook of my arm, which started me giggling. I patted her head, heaving with desperate attempts to hold in the giggles, while Scarlett snickered into my armpit.

The situation was funnier than the joke. I managed to pull a straight face long enough to see the mourners turn back to the graveside, press hands with the bereaved, and tut-tut at our behaviour. I promptly swung Scarlett around and marched her out of the church grounds, where we allowed ourselves to give in to the giggles. We wiped our eyes, sobered up, and leaned against the mossy, sodden stone wall surrounding the graveyard.

'It wasn't even that funny.'

'You should have seen their faces.'

'We'll be the talk of the town.'

'Let them talk.'

I could smell whatever soap Scarlett used, the shampoo sheen beneath the salt tang of rain in her hair, faintly perfumed moisturiser. There were tears of laughter on the collar of my shirt. I brushed them off.

'Did you talk to Pearse?'

'Of course I did.'

'And?'

'Come on.'

She took my arm. We walked towards town. I knew that I wouldn't see her again for a very long time – perhaps ever. I tried to breathe in the scent of her skin, and failed.

'Pearse will have the van ready for you when you need it. This is his number.'

She pressed a piece of paper into my hand. Her fingers were as delicate as the straws of hay in your hair on a summer's day, but it was best to forget about everything I'd have to leave behind. I already knew there was no turning back, and that meant saying goodbye to the people I loved.

'My bank details are on there as well. Don't put it all in at once.'

'I know.'

'Thank you,' she whispered, stood on tiptoe to kiss my cheek, and was gone.

I didn't turn to watch her leave, but watched the church instead, where the first lot of mourners were trickling out. I watched them until the sound of Scarlett's heels clicking on the pavement was drowned out by the sombre bongs of the church bell, which evaporated in the air like ripples on water. One thing I wouldn't miss was the sound of church bells, the smell of incense and hypocrisy, the stone cold emptiness of religious ceremony.

What would it take to break the Catholic Church's stranglehold on births, deaths and marriages?

Everyone knew about the years of abuse suffered by children at the hands of predatory priests. Everyone knew about the slave labour sapped out of women whose babies were taken from them, abused, sold, or tossed into mass graves. Everyone knew that religion was an insurance scam, but still we went through the motions, paying lip service to a bunch of sexist homophobes in drag, while they conspired to run a worldwide paedophile ring.

As the playwright said, 'The more things a man is ashamed of, the more respectable he is.'

You've only got to look at the corruption of the Church to know what he was on about. The thing is, none of the people I loved were what you'd call respectable. We didn't care what the neighbours said. We didn't watch each other through twitching curtains. We don't have a facade to maintain, because we live our lives out loud. We might be unpolished, or rude, or vulgar, but we're real. We're not pretending to be any better than we are, so you can fuck off with your scented candles and your summertime barbeques, your front-row seats at Mass and your tickets to the opera, your Sunday supplements and your carbon-footprint anxiety.

I'd been thinking long and hard about how to disappear completely. If this was going to work, I had to tear down the fabric of my own cocooned existence. I'd worked out all the things I'd have to leave behind. I'd be kissing goodbye to university, my small circle of friends, the certain knowledge of always having a roof over my head. No more iPhone, no more Facebook, no more credit cards. That was how people got caught when they went on the run, but clung to their old lives.

I stood watching the mourners trickle through the streets. Even Muck McGinley had been loved. The camera crews buzzed around me as if I wasn't there. A news reporter stood with her back to the church and recorded a rehearsed spiel on the aftermath of the murder, while behind her, teenage boys gurned for the camera, grinning and punching each other on the arms, waving to an imaginary audience.

A helicopter flew by overhead, and one of the crew yelled, 'Cut!'

The news reporter swore.

'How much longer do we have to hang around this dump? I can't even get a latte.'

'Take it from the top. We need the mourners in the shot.'

A small boy tore the leaves off a white carnation, most likely from a funeral wreath. He traipsed after his mother, tripping over his shoelaces as she wiped the tracks of tears from her face. She nodded at me. I nodded back. Maybe she didn't recognise me, but only saw someone who stood facing the crowd, and wasn't a part of it.

The leaves floated into the gutter, danced on water, and disappeared.

14

Double-cross

Everything is different in the early hours of the morning. The silence is softer. The shadows are deeper. The roaming gangs of drunken youths have fallen apart. Junkies stop creeping like zombies from alleyways. Winos are passed out in doorways, clutching bottles wrapped in brown paper, their bodies wrapped in tatters. Prostitutes have deserted the roadsides, taking their pushed-up tits and hitched-up skirts home until tomorrow. Men cruising by moonlight for sex have gone home to their wives. Twenty-four-hour convenience stores hum only with neon, depressed staff, and half-asleep customers. Internet cafés buzz only with geeks in headphones playing shoot-'em-ups with gamers across the globe. Offices and factories dream.

It's quiet, and it's dark.

I had set my alarm for 3 AM, the time when, statistically, most people are in bed. It didn't matter. Firstly, I hadn't slept, so setting my alarm had been pointless. Secondly, you can't trust statistics to predict the behaviour of individuals. 3 AM sounds like a good time to perform clandestine operations, but there's always the risk of the unexpected.

What if somebody's wife suddenly went into labour, and he carried her to their car, and in his haste to get out of the driveway, ran over the night-time jogger with his headphones on? What if a crying baby woke the woman next door, who fumbled for a cigarette, and struck a match, not realising that her husband had gassed himself in the kitchen two hours ago, and the whole house exploded? What if a lonely woman out walking her dog was standing at the very spot where her lover had jilted her fifteen years ago, which just happened to be the very same spot and the very same night that I'd chosen to swap one white van for another white van?

What were the odds? I didn't know. All I could do was stick to the plan and hope for the best.

I took the handgun out of the shoebox stashed beneath my bed, slid home a clip of six bullets, and tested its weight in my hand. It would do.

My luggage was packed. I believe in travelling light. I had the documents Frank had prepared for me, a birth certificate and passport in the name of Thomas James McKeever.

'Your real name is your middle name, in case you make any slip-ups.'

I had a new birthday. May, 5th, 1991.

'You're a Taurus. A bull!'

What Frank didn't know was that I had other documents too. I'd made a trip to Aunty Kate's, to help her go through Duncan's things. we 'd sat in her living room sipping tea and eating Kit Kats, while she'd leafed through photo albums, sighing and reminiscing.

When Aunty Kate went out to freshen the pot, I'd rifled through the box of papers and found Duncan's passport, unstamped, his birth certificate, tattered and torn but intact, and, after a heart attack or two, his National Insurance Number card. I'd pocketed all three, Aunty Kate none the wiser.

The plan was clear in my mind. I would swap vans with Pearse Mahon tonight, as agreed. I would leave the real van, the murder van, behind. I would drive the substitute van to England under the name of Thomas James McKeever, meet my contact there, get the money, and disappear. Neither Thomas James McKeever nor Jay O'Reilly would ever be heard of again. I would travel to some obscure part of England and check into a hotel or a B & B. Somewhere anonymous, until I found my feet.

Meanwhile, the murder van would be found. This was the tricky part. It had to be hidden until I'd reached England and got the money, but found after I'd disappeared.

It was a difficult one. I'd had a brainwave. I'd gone, of course, to Martin.

'I know you don't want to call the cops about the van.'

'Damn fucking right I don't.'

'How about this, then? If I tell you what night I'm swapping the vans, and where, can you do me a favour?'

'It depends.'

'Go to the area the next day at six in the evening. Start a fire, not at the van, but near it. I'll leave enough stuff lying around to get the fire going – rubber, wood, petrol, matches. No, bring your own matches, in case it rains. Then, the fire brigade will have to come to put the fire out, they'll see the van, and the cops will be called.'

'You're sure that'll work?'

'It'll work.'

'What if it's found earlier, not by the cops?'

'Then text me, as planned. You'd hear about it, you know you would.'

'I'm scared.'

'You'll be fine.'

'I'm scared for you.'

'Don't worry about me.'

Then Martin had hugged me unexpectedly. I broke away, embarrassed.

'I'll do it,' Martin had muttered, staring at the ground.

'Good man.'

I was going to miss Martin, but I wondered if he'd miss me more.

Once I was safe, I would become Duncan Goodman. I had his ID. Duncan would not be using it. No one in England knew whether Duncan Goodman, born December 12th 1993 and holder of an Irish passport, was dead or alive. There was a reasonable enough resemblance for me to pass as the pale-skinned, dark-haired, blue-eyed man in his photo. Yeah, so I'd put on some muscle in the six years since the photo had been taken, but who really looked like their passport photo anyway? Haha. Very true. Thank you, sir.

Most importantly, with Duncan's National Insurance Number, I could work when I needed to, or claim social benefits. I was, having been born in one of the six counties, a dual citizen of the Republic of Ireland, and also the United Kingdom of Great Britain and Northern Ireland. I was a subject of the Queen, not an immigrant. I'd been resident in the Republic of Ireland until recently, but had moved to England, what with the recession and everything, yeah? Yeah. It would probably be best to take up a casual job in a small town, rather than draw the dole. I didn't want social services asking too many questions. And if I saw anyone I knew, I'd scarper. The beauty of travelling light was that everything you needed to get on with your life could fit in one sports bag – socks and jocks, a change of jeans, a few T-shirts, a jacket, toothbrush, deodorant, and your documentation.

And the handgun.

Both my parents, of course, knew that tonight was the night. They ought now to be sound asleep. I dressed, grabbed the bag and the gun, walked downstairs and out the door. I allowed my eyes to adjust to the darkness, breathing in the silence. I crossed the garden and hopped the fence. The murder van was stashed in one of Frank's outhouses.

Cold sweat trickled down my spine.

Clouds were drawn back from the full moon.

The only sound was my footsteps.

The van shone like a ghost in the dark.

I opened the door on the driver's side, and hesitated. Stupid, the way the mind plays tricks. I had half expected – what? To sense the dead man's spirit wailing from the back of the van? Muck McGinley had never even been in the fucking thing.

I slid into the driver's seat, stuck the keys in the ignition, and revved up. The van purred to life. My biggest concern was that Monaghan was watching the premises. I'd staked out the land earlier that day, and seen nothing. It was time to put the plan into action.

The plan had been to drive the van straight to the ferry, where passage had been booked under my assumed name. The plan now was to take a detour to scrubland where Pearse Mahon would have already stashed the substitute van. We were going to split the money fifty-fifty, on the condition he spent it on Scarlett and Alison.

If I was caught now . . .

There was no sign of the cops. I drove to the scrubland in no time at all. I did the last half-mile over an open field. I parked at the far corner of the scrubland as arranged, and got out. The field I'd driven through was a tangle of trees, bracken, and overgrown hedgerow.

It was a good place to lose something. Further along the hedge, under a thrown together canopy of branches and tarpaulin, was the substitute van. Pearse Mahon had kept his word.

'Money talks.'

I got to work.

I put on gloves, and wiped my fingerprints from the keys, steering wheel, gearstick and door of the murder van. I wiped down the seat I'd sat in, in case I'd shed any hairs or skin onto it. Then I planted hairs from Frank's pillow and fibres from his clothes in the front of the van. I'd lifted Frank's thumbprint from a glass with some Sellotape, which I'd kept fresh by sticking one end of the piece to the other, making a loop. I took it from the breast pocket of my shirt, unpeeled the loop, and pressed the thumbprint on to the front panel of the glove compartment.

That ought to be enough to place Frank in the murder van, which in turn ought to be enough to search our home and land on suspicion of murder, conspiracy and fraud.

Next, I made the guts of a bonfire with the tarpaulin and branches that Pearse had used to conceal the substitute van. I set it just far enough away from the hedge. I doused it with petrol, threw the tin on top, peeled off my gloves, and stuffed them into the heart of the bonfire-to-be.

I checked the van that Pearse had provided. Same make, same model, same plates. Perfect. I got inside.

I had a sudden panic. Was the murder van too visible? Should I put some branches around it? No. No, it had to look abandoned, rather than hidden.

What I hoped for, what should happen, was that the cops would assume that the bonfire, which would catch the attention of the authorities, had been intended to consume the van which had been used in the kidnapping and murder.

I fished the keys out from the sunshade where Pearse had said I'd find them, and put the engine key in the ignition. I didn't turn the key.

The moonlight had turned the scrubland grey. Everything was flat and shadowless.

My hands trembled on the steering wheel. I looked in the mirror on the back of the sunshade just as I had the morning of Duncan's wake, and saw a vein throbbing in my temple. My eyes were still anxious. My palms were still sweaty. I needed a fucking cigarette.

I turned the key.

The engine growled.

The headlights sprang to life, drowning out the pale moonlight in a sulphuric flush of yellow which spread throughout the scrubland in front of me.

Something stirred, faintly, beyond the reach of the headlights. It glided towards me, silently, from the gloom.

Into the light, a figure sprang to life, bent over handlebars, pushing towards me, panting, wild.

Martin.

He jumped off the bike and ran towards me.

'He's coming.'

'What?'

'Your dad. He's coming.'

'How—'

'I saw you. From my house. He followed you. For fuck's sake, Jay, get out of here!'

'I don't—'

'I was watching from my house,' Martin yelled. He grabbed my shirt. I stood there, mute and stupid.

'I was watching to make sure this didn't happen. But it did. You came down the road. Your dad followed, in his jeep. He's—'

'He's here.'

The jeep, headlights off, smashed through the hedge, tearing up the scrubland.

'Go!'

I pushed Martin aside.

I reached for my gun.

A shot rang out.

Martin crumpled to the ground as the jeep bounced to a halt, black blood spilling on the dead grey grass.

15

Standoff

There was no time to check if Martin was alive or dead. I stood behind the van's door, as Frank's monstrous bulk swung out of the jeep, gun in hand. He lowered his weapon as he stepped forward, out of the immediate glare of the headlights.

'Stupid, keeping the lights on.'

I stepped out from behind the van door.

'I was just about to leave when Martin got here.'

'Who is he, your boyfriend?'

'A friend.'

'How sweet. My son made friends with the town cocksucker.'

'Fuck you.'

'Oh, you have. You fucking killed me. I did this for you, made money for you, raised you right, and you repaid me by turning your back on us, then betraying me the minute I give you my trust.'

We stood face to face, fingers curled on triggers, identical masks of fury on our faces.

Neither of us flinched.

'You know how come I'm here?'

'You never trusted me?'

'Your pal Pearse Mahon ratted you out, that's why. You

stupid fuck. What did you think would happen? He came straight to me and told me what you had planned. You know what you should've done? Told him it was a coup. Told him you were planning on retiring me, then taking over the business. Then maybe the greedy little bastard would've gone along with it. But you kick the shit out of him, then you expect him to put his balls on the chopping block for money he can make off jacking a few cars? You're out of your mind. You're sick in the head. I'd be doing you a favour.'

Frank's gun swung up level to my chest.

'You know what the real killer is? I knew this was coming. I knew you'd break my heart. I offered you a chance to make it up to me, because I knew you wouldn't take it, you ungrateful little fuck.'

Frank's free paw struck his chest, above his heart.

I laughed.

'You think this is funny? What's so fucking funny? Being shot dead in a field by your old man is funny to you now, is it?'

'Fucking hilarious.'

'Why?'

'You set me up. You set me up to take the bait and fuck you over, just to prove what a shit son I am. That's hysterical.'

'I'm not laughing.'

'You don't think it's funny that you set me up to fail? That's what you've done all my life.'

'I gave you everything.'

'You gave me fuck-all.'

'So it's my fault you're a loser, yeah? It's my fault you've got a shitty job, and no woman to keep your dick wet, and you got to run around with faggots for company? Get on the fucking couch, tell the doctor how Daddy was a bad man. Boo-hoo. At least I am a man, what the fuck are you?'

'Yeah, that's right. I'm not man enough to steal from other people. I'm not clever enough to rob the country blind, with my counterfeit factories and laundered money. I'm not man enough to hire a gang of hoods to beat up a woman and shoot her boyfriend in the back of the head. Wow. You must be proud.'

'You bet your fucking life I'm proud,' Frank said, teeth glistening, gun still trained on my chest. 'Why don't you keep on talking? Maybe I'll bury you beside your gay boyfriend.'

Martin's blood, black beneath the moonlight, trickled to the sole of my shoe.

'Smugglers used to be rebels,' I said. 'They used to have a cause. What are they now? What are you, Dad? You're just a grubby little businessman with bloody hands. You don't love this country. Your whole way of life depends on keeping it ripped up the middle. You're broken,' I said, tapping the throbbing vein in my temple, 'and it's too late to fix you. You're going to put a bullet in my heart because I wanted to put right all the things you've done wrong.'

'Let's be clear about this,' Frank said, cocking the gun a little higher. 'I'm putting a bullet in your heart because you were willing to turn me over to the cops.'

Frank's hand was steady. His hand was curled around the gun as naturally as a baboon held a banana. The image was ridiculous. This time, I didn't feel like laughing.

I was spent.

Something rustled over my shoulder.

Martin?

'You know what the best part is?' Frank said. 'You could have had all this, if you wanted it. I could have given it to you.'

'You never wanted me to be in your gang.'

'You never asked.'

'You never offered.'

'I gave you every chance.'

A car, somewhere in the distance, drove out of earshot.

What were the odds of someone happening to come along and rescue me?

I didn't know, but the odds weren't in my favour.

We were alone.

No coincidences would save me now.

'You think I'm evil? Bullshit. I know who I am. I'm running a racket that makes a lot of money for someone like me, and I don't stick my nose in politics, or charity, or humanitarian aid, because believe me, that shit is as corrupt as any scam I've got going on. More so, because I'm not pretending to do this for the poor, poor people of war-torn Northern Ireland. I give people work, and they work hard, and I take the flack if it all goes tits up. But I won't let it go tits up, see? All I got to do is hold it together, and everything ticks over, nice and easy. My boys earn their wages. The cops earn their wages. And every taxpayer misses a penny in their pocket every week. So what? They can make it all back a hundred times over by buying my cigarettes and diesel. So cut the bleeding heart bullshit, you two-faced cunt. I gave you a chance. If you weren't up for the job, you never should've said yes to me.'

From the corner of my eye, I saw Martin's finger twitch.

If Frank knew he was alive, he'd put a bullet in his head. *Lie still. Shut up.*

If I could distract Frank, Martin might still get out of this alive.

'What about Muck McGinley? Tortured? Why? What for?'

'That fuck.' Frank spat in the grass, and I saw a flash of McGinley's brains splattering the ground.

'What was I supposed to do? Those moronic kids of his were running around, beating up my men, all over my turf. You know what? If I was half the monster you think I am, I would've splattered both those kids' brains all over the other one's cock. But I didn't, did I? You know why? Coz it was their father's fault. So Daddy got it in the skull, and yeah, I let him know why. Why shouldn't I? The kids got a free pass, coz I'm nice that way. He ought to be thanking me from his grave.'

'It was wrong.'

'No, what's wrong is turning your old man in to the cops after years of turning your back on your family, because you didn't get the life you thought you deserved, you spoilt fuck.'

Martin moaned from the ditch.

Shut up. He'll kill you too. Shut up.

Everything I'd wanted to believe was wrong. I'd imagined the afterlife as one great story, and imagined everyone's story as a cinematic masterpiece of their own creation. If the afterlife was anything like I'd imagined it to be, then it would affirm the lie that we were masters of our own destiny, because real life was just as I'd imagined it too. It wasn't a story. It didn't have a narrative. There were no heroes. There'd be no neat resolution to my tale. There'd be a mess, and a waste of a life. You made mistakes, and you paid for them.

At least I'd tried, right?

Right.

I'd tried.

I'd tried to take the one chance I'd got to make a tiny corner of the universe more fair, and I'd fucked it up.

'Anything you'd like to get off your chest?'

If everyone tried to look out for just one other person in the world, wouldn't it be a better place? If each of us tackled the one thing we knew was wrong in our lives, the one thing we could fix, wouldn't everyone's life be better?

Fuck it.

'No.'

Time slowed down to my last breath of cold, morning air, as Frank hefted his gun.

I'd kill for a fucking cigarette.

'Stop!' Martin yelled.

Frank's eyes flickered.

Bang.

Frank's jaw fell. He crumpled to his knees. His gun dropped to the ground as he tumbled over. A figure toting a shotgun appeared from behind his toppled corpse, glowing amber around the edges from the headlights of the van. Dolores stepped over her husband's body with a grimace, and put her arms around me, holding me tight as I shivered in the cold.

16

The Organised Criminal

A trickle of blood ran from Frank's open mouth, while a pool of the stuff flooded from the hole in his back. He looked pitiable in death. Martin dragged himself up from the ground and staggered towards us, as we stood, arms around one another, looking down at the body.

'I'm bleeding to death here.'

I ripped open Martin's tattered T-shirt to reveal the bullet wound in his shoulder.

'It fucking hurts.'

'Clean wound,' Dolores said. 'Missed your heart, if you have one, and – let's see – it's lodged inside. Looks like it missed the bone, too. You were lucky.'

'I've been passed out in my own blood and piss for God knows how long.'

'Some people pay good money for that sort of thing.'

'Knock it off. I need to get to the hospital.'

'I'll call someone who can take care of it for you, no questions asked.'

'No way. Jay, call me an ambulance.'

'I wouldn't do that,' Dolores said. 'I'm a better shot than Frank was.'

Martin's teeth chattered as he stared at the oozing heap of flesh at our feet.

'So what do we do now?'

'First things first,' Dolores said. 'Kill the lights. It's like a bloody circus out here.'

I did as I was told.

'How did you find us, mum?'

'I followed your father when he went after you. I told him I was taking a sleeping pill, so he thought I was out for the count. Not on your life. I guessed what you were up to when Pearse Mahon wanted a hush-hush with your father. Poor man. You broke his heart.'

'And you shot him.'

'Be grateful.'

There was a silence. Moonlight ran its fingers through the treetops and the grass, caressing cooling metal and flesh, raising goosebumps on my arms. Martin sat down cross-legged in the dirt, cradling his left shoulder with his right hand.

'I'm sorry,' I said.

'You should be. Where was I? Yes. Your father followed you. I was prepared for it. I snuck down after him and followed him in my car. I kept the lights off. It was easy to do, with town so quiet. I saw you on your bicycle,' Dolores said with a nod at Martin, 'and had to stop to let you get ahead. I hoped you might buy me some time, although I must say, I thought you'd be dead by the time I got here. Well done, you.'

'Thanks.'

'I parked my car down the road, loaded the shotgun, and crept up behind your father in time to hear your parting argument. Men are so stupid.'

I wiped tears from my face with clumsy hands.

'Don't, darling, don't. Ssshhh. Don't cry.'

Dolores put her arm around me. I collapsed onto her, sobbing silently.

'Didn't you love him?' Martin asked, nodding at Frank's body.

'Of course I did,' Dolores said. 'I married him. We raised a son together. Don't get me wrong, I love money and power as much as anyone, but not more than you, Jay, not more than my baby.'

She stroked my hair like a child.

Blood trickled through Martin's fingers.

Frank's body stopped bleeding.

'How could you do this, mum? How could you do this, and be so calm?'

'You don't know the half of it. Now come along, we've got work to do. We've got to clean up this mess, and look after your friend.'

'Martin.'

'Dolores. Pleased to meet you. You two aren't – are you?'

'Jesus, mum.'

'No, we're not fucking, which is just as well, seeing as how I'm about to expire at your son's feet.'

'Oh, quit whining. Jay, give him your jacket, see if you can staunch the wound. Not too tight, you don't want to cut off blood flow to the arm.'

I took a bottle of water from the van and poured it over Martin's ripped-open shoulder, exposing the entry wound and torn flesh around it. Then I took off my jacket and wound it under Martin's armpit and over the wound.

I looked down at my bloody hands.

'Just like old times.'

Martin looked at the blood trickling between his fingers. 'Just like love.'

With his forefinger, Martin smeared blood across my lips.

I licked it off.

'Salty.'

'Almost done,' Dolores said, tossing the words over her shoulder from Frank's jeep. 'Weapons, petrol, bonfire, money . . .'

'Mum? What did you mean, when you said I didn't know the half of it?'

'I don't know what you're talking about. Now, can Martin walk?'

'He'll be fine. Tell me. What did you mean?'

Martin and I were huddled together in the grass, smeared in blood and shivering in the chill night air.

Dolores sighed.

'Well, I suppose it makes no difference, now.'

Dolores came over and sat beside us. She pulled a strand of hair from her eyes and tucked it behind an ear. She stared off somewhere over Martin's aching shoulder.

'You know what your cousin Duncan was like. He was a goon. He couldn't hold his drink and had a tendency to blabber. Your father was getting worried. What if the cops got him on something fairly minor – a stolen car, say, or enough drugs to prosecute for intent to supply? He might flip. One day in a cell without booze and he'd say anything for a drink. You know he would. It wouldn't do. I began to think the man would be better off dead, and when I heard what your father had planned, I thought, well, what's the harm?'

'What did he have planned?'

'A bullet in the back of the head. Typical of your father. No finesse, and a bit nasty. He thought it would serve as a good warning to everyone else in the crew. I tried to raise the matter delicately, you know, how would his kids cope if anything were to happen to Duncan? He said they'd be taken care of, that we had plenty of money put aside for a rainy day. I said, wasn't that what the insurance company was for? And your father said, well, no, probably not, not if there were any suspicious circumstances surrounding the death. You see, he actively wanted suspicious circumstances, to keep the rest of the crew on their toes. That seemed unfair. And what about me?'

'What about you?'

'Well, why should I pay for Duncan's family, if he came to a sticky end? How lovely, I thought, if Duncan were to die a nice, natural death, before your father got his hands on him.'

'But he did, mum. He died of drink.'

'Yes, of course he did. It was acute liver failure following alcohol poisoning. The silly man literally drank himself to death. But where do you think he got the booze from?'

We stared at Dolores in disbelief.

She smiled.

'I bought a crate of whiskey and drove it over to that sad little room he was living in. I told him it was a present from Frank, in gratitude for all the work he'd put in over the years. Would he like a snifter to celebrate? Well, of course he would. We sat down together – I had to move a plate of mouldy Spam out of my way, disgusting – and cracked open a bottle. I didn't drink as much as he thought. I let him talk, and one bottle led to another, and another. God, it was boring. He even tried it on with me, can you believe it? Cheek. Luckily, he could barely lift his drinking arm by the end, never mind his dick. And I let him drink, and drink, and drink, and once he'd passed out, I poured another bottle down his throat for good measure, and left, leaving just one last bottle of whiskey behind for good luck. And it worked, didn't it? Because he died.'

'But poor Aunty Kate . . .'

'He was a disgrace. Never mind, the insurance company paid out, and we didn't have to give a penny to that lousy wife of his.'

Dolores stood up, slapping her hands together smartly, as if washing them clean.

'Now, let's get this little job over with.'

I staggered to my feet, dragging Martin with me.

'I can't believe it,' I said.

'Believe it,' Martin said.

'Help me roll your father's body over to the bonfire,' Dolores said, gritting her teeth under Frank's dead weight. 'I've put my shotgun and Frank's handgun into the middle of it. They won't burn, obviously, but it should destroy any DNA evidence.'

'Why are we burning his body?'

'The wound is in his back. If there's no evidence of a shot-gun wound, they may not be able to prove it was murder. Of course, there may be some bone damage they can prove was a rear-entry bullet wound, but I doubt it. I'm really a very good shot. Heave ho.'

Martin watched us roll Frank's body to the bonfire. Dolores took the matches from my trembling hand. We watched the match spark and burst to life between her painted nails, watched her toss the match to the petrol-soaked pile, and saw the flames leap, licking wood, tarpaulin, and Frank's body.

Dolores flipped open her phone.

'Darling, it's me. I've got an emergency. House call.'

Dolores reeled off Martin's address, which shouldn't have surprised us.

'Get home,' Dolores said to Martin. 'You'll be taken care of. I don't need to tell you that if one word of this gets out—'

'It won't.'

'Jay. This is important. Look at me. Look away from the flames, Jay, look at me. You must get away. Take the ferry, like you were supposed to. Do not deliver the van to that man, do you hear me? He'll have heard of this by then. Do you hear me?'

'I hear you.'

'I don't know what you'll do when you get to England, but you won't be able to use the name your father arranged for you once you land there and ditch the van. Got it? Do you understand?'

'I've thought of that. I took Duncan's passport and ID. I can live under his name – for a while, at least.'

'Darling, I'm very proud of you. That really was clever.'

She hugged me tightly, unaware that my eyes were staring blindly into nothingness. She let me go, fishing a packet of cigarettes from her pocket.

'Cigarette?'

I nodded.

She lit up off the bonfire, lit one for me and one for her. I sucked it hungrily, like an infant on the breast.

'One more thing before we go.'

Dolores walked over to the spot from which she'd first appeared behind Frank. The flames from the bonfire were spat and hissed, throwing light and shadow amok like demons. There was a suitcase on the ground. Dolores picked it up.

'I brought this, as well as the shotgun. It's for you. One hundred thousand pounds.'

I took the suitcase from her, opened it up, and stared at the stacks of crisp twenty-pound notes inside.

'He was becoming reckless, Jay. He was out of control. Somebody had to step in and take over. It's my business now, and I'll take good care of it. Call me when you're safe. Get out of here, now. Go. I love you. Disappear.'

Dolores kissed me on the cheek and hugged me tight.

I just stood there, mute, staring at the money in the suit-case.

'Make sure he gets out of here in one piece,' Dolores said to Martin.

'I will.'

'Go.'

'I just need a minute,' I said, 'to say goodbye.'

'I understand.'

With a final squeeze of my arm, Dolores turned her back on us, setting off across scrubland to her car, her empty home, her new life.

Everything had changed.

I was not the organised criminal I thought I had become.

I laughed.

'What's so funny?'

Oh, how I laughed.

'Jay? You heard her. Get out of here, man. Take the van and get out of here.'

I turned around, a stupid smile on my face, the suitcase full of money open in my arms. I dropped it with a thud. The money bounced. Flames danced as Martin's eyes lit up.

I stooped down, scooping up handfuls of cash, and began to toss them, wad by wad, into the bonfire.

'Jay! What the fuck? Take the money, and get the fuck away!'

I ripped open the paper bands sealing the wads of cash, and tossed the notes into the air. The money fluttered through moonlight, smoke, and flames, catching sparks, catching fire, beginning to burn in mid-air before falling into the maw of the bonfire, which reeked of burning flesh, as my dad was consumed, inch by fatty inch, by the fire which had already eaten through his clothes, his hair, the first layers of skin.

Martin grabbed me with his one good hand and yelled.

'Stop it! Take it! Go!'

I pushed him aside, gathering more money for the fire.

The tip of my cigarette glowed as I worked, smoke pouring from my nostrils.

I peeled one twenty from a wad, lifted it to the tip of my cigarette, and watched as it burned between my fingers.

'Fuck this.'

Martin grabbed as much cash as he could, shoving it in every pocket. I carried on chucking money on the funeral pyre. Martin turned – lungs churning, shoulder weeping blood, pockets full of twenties – and ran all the way home.

About the Author

Jarlath Gregory grew up in Crossmaglen, County Armagh. He is the author of *Snapshots* (Sitric, 2001) and *G.A.A.Y: One Hundred Ways to Love a Beautiful Loser* (Sitric, 2005). He lives in Dublin.